Broken Lens

VIBE a Steamy Romance
Series #3

Broken Lens

Lynn Chantale

4 Horsemen
Publications, Inc.

Broken Lens
VIBE a Steamy Romance Series #3
Copyright © 2021 Lynn Chantale. All rights reserved.

4 Horsemen
Publications, Inc.

4 Horsemen Publications, Inc.
1497 Main St. Suite 169
Dunedin, FL 34698
4horsemenpublications.com
info@4horsemenpublications.com

Cover by 4HP
Typesetting by MC
Editor Muñeca Fossette

All rights to the work within are reserved to the author and publisher. No part of this publication may be reproduced, stored in a retrieval system, or transmitted in any form or by any means, electronic, mechanical, photocopying, recording, scanning, or otherwise, except as permitted under Section 107 or 108 of the 1976 International Copyright Act, without prior written permission except in brief quotations embodied in critical articles and reviews. Please contact either the Publisher or Author to gain permission.

This is book is meant as a reference guide. All characters, organizations, and events portrayed in this novel are either products of the author's imagination or are used fictitiously. All brands, quotes, and cited work respectfully belongs to the original rights holders and bear no affiliation to the authors or publisher.

Library of Congress Control Number: 2021948564

Print ISBN: 978-1-64450-438-3
Audio ISBN: 978-1-64450-436-9
Ebook ISBN: 978-1-64450-437-6

Table of Contents

Chapter One 1
Chapter Two 15
Chapter Three 29
Chapter Four 35
Chapter Five 47
Chapter Six 53
Chapter Seven 66
Chapter Eight 70
Chapter Nine 73
Chapter Ten 80
Chapter Eleven 87
Epilogue 98
Author's Note 101

Chapter One

Serefina Gellar bounced with barely controlled excitement. Finally, she was getting a chance to meet her idol, a woman she'd followed on every social platform she could find. Why fawn over the likes of Lil Nas X, H.E.R, or Lizzo when she had the biggest sensation, Geneva, in her backyard.

Did it matter that Geneva was born without eyes? Serefina looked up Anophthalmia. It was a condition causing a baby to be born without one or both of its eyes. Geneva even spoke about it on her website. Something like one in over a half million babies was affected. And Geneva presented it like everything else on her website, with grace and humor. Serefina loved following Geneva's exploits on TikTok, Instagram, and YouTube. Wherever Geneva was, Serefina followed. And now she was going to meet Geneva in person.

Serefina clutched a notebook in one hand and her phone in the other. The day was perfect. Blue skies, bright sunshine, and a cool breeze kept everything pleasant. For a moment, she focused on her surroundings. Picnic tables were lined in three neat rows beneath a tent erected for the occasion. Not far from the picnic area was a row of ten or twelve outdoor bathrooms. As a general rule, Serefina didn't like Porta Potties, but the ones for this event were rather nice. The bathrooms were well lit, ventilated, and had sinks with hot and cold water. She had checked the bathrooms because she wanted to make sure she looked perfect when she met Geneva.

Serefina tucked a lock of wavy, newly dyed, brown hair behind her ear. She had tried to get Geneva's exact shade, but it seemed darker than Geneva's. Serefina was intent on having the same hair color as Geneva when they finally took a selfie together.

Of course, she'd have to do something about the way her hair curled. She'd never seen Geneva with curly hair. Geneva Had to have been born with impossibly straight hair. Serefina would have to ask what products Geneva used.

The phone buzzed in her hand. She nearly dropped the device in her haste to view the notification. Oh. My. God. Geneva was live!

Serefina searched the area, moving past clowns, a DJ booth, and lines of people waiting for cotton candy or popcorn. Beyond the crowd, in front of the dunk tank, an old man was taunting spectators. A petite woman stood in front of a table beneath a banner heralding "White Cane Awareness."

She fanned her hand, willing the sudden tears not to fall. She was really here. In the same park. Just feet from Geneva. Serefina forced down excitement, pocketed her phone, and moved toward the pretty, dark-haired woman.

As Serefina drew closer, she caught better glimpses of Geneva's flawlessly white sundress. Bright blue cornflowers edged the hem and bodice of the ankle-length dress.

Matching strappy, flat, blue sandals adorned her feet. Even the sparkly polish on Geneva's toes matched.

A couple of silver bangles ringed her arm and chimed together whenever she moved her hands. She talked with her hands, gesturing as if conducting a choir. The movements were delicate and graceful. Serefina paused to take in her beauty. She reveled in being close enough to touch Geneva and breathe the same air.

Serefina pressed a hand to her pounding heart. She was in the presence of greatness.

"How was that?" The slight lisp which would've sounded childish on anyone else only added to Geneva's charm.

"Great. You had like a hundred people tuned in for those few minutes."

It wasn't until he spoke that Serefina noticed the tall, gangly man with the dome-shaped afro. His trimmed sideburns were so sharply and neatly lined, they could've been painted on. When he smiled, his neat, little mustache smiled too. Serefina recognized him as Geneva's husband. His milk chocolate skin was a smooth contrast to Geneva's peaches and cream complexion.

A momentary stab of jealousy curdled her gut and forced a frown. Here were two beautiful people, and Serefina had to go home to a dumpy drunk. Now, if she had a man like Geneva's husband, life would be so much better. For now, she would content herself with meeting Geneva.

"Oh god. Oh god, oh god. I'm such a huge fan," Serefina exclaimed as she rushed forward. "I follow everything you do, and I'm just a huge fan, and you inspire me with what you do."

Shifting to face Serefina, Geneva smiled. "Oh, thank you."

Up close, Geneva was prettier than any of her online pictures. Serefina could see the bit of eyeshadow behind the gray lenses of Geneva's sunglasses.

"I really can't believe I'm getting a chance to meet you."

Geneva laughed. "You're so sweet to think so. I just like to take pictures and talk to people."

Serefina still couldn't believe she was standing in front of her idol. She was a good four inches taller than Geneva, but Geneva's presence made her seem tall. And she smelled as good as she looked—like plums and honey. With trembling hands, Serefina held out her notebook.

"Could I have your autograph?"

A blush stole into her cheeks. *Wow? Really?* Geneva pulled a small, plastic card from her pocket. An inch wide opening ran the length of the card.

Serefina stared at the card a moment before she took it. She opened to a fresh page in her book, placed the card on the page, and carefully placed the book in Geneva's hands.

She was touching her idol. *Oh god, oh god, oh god, oh god*. Was this the best day of her life or what?

"What is this called?" she asked as she watched Geneva form each letter.

"A signature guide."

"You want a photo of this for your website?" the man asked.

"Would it be all right?" Geneva asked, handing back the pen and paper but keeping the signature guide.

"I'd love to," Serefina replied.

Geneva wrapped an arm around Serefina's waist. Serefina thought she was going to faint. Her idol was holding her as if they were old friends, as if they were best buds.

"Looks great, ladies," the man said.

"Could-could I have a copy of the photo?" asked Serefina.

A few seconds later, Serefina stared from the signature to the photo to the signature and back again. She had met, had a conversation with, and touched Geneva Martin. She had a picture with Geneva Martin. And now, she was going to do everything in her power to make Geneva's life her own.

⁓

Here they were again, all gathered like they were such good friends. Mr. VIP curled his lip as he subtly sneered at Penelope. He'd almost gotten her with his little makeshift bomb. *And if the snake had gotten Amelia.* He sighed. At least he had his consolation prizes. Two small business owners were dead and gone.

He suppressed the giggle bubbling from his gut. Instead, he allowed a cruel little smile to crease his lips. He would get retribution.

Could he call it that? What was he doing? It wasn't vengeance, or maybe it was. *No.* He shook his head. He wasn't avenging anything. He was exterminating and eradicating the city of the overachieving blind people. *Successful, disabled people were the scourge of humanity. Why couldn't they sit down somewhere and fade into the blackness?*

He clenched his hands at his sides. *They were the reason he couldn't get where he wanted. They were the reason his business failed. Each of the overcoming, independent, blind people milling around at this stupid event was the reason he had failed.*

Bleating horns cut through his reverie. A black idea formulated in his brain as he watched vehicles whiz back and forth in a blur of color.

It would be easy to shove someone into oncoming traffic with all the blind and visually impaired people meandering around.

Yes. How easy it would be indeed.

―――

"Tilt left," the mechanical voice instructed. "Two faces located near bottom, right-hand corner."

Geneva Martin bit her lip as she concentrated on her phone. She listened, making adjustments as the voice prompted.

"Camera level."

She double-tapped the take-picture icon, and the phone's camera feature clicked several times.

"Thanks, guys," she said, slipping the device in her pocket. "This will look great on my blog."

"Anytime, Geneva," said the cheerful, masculine voice. "There are some other members on the council here. I think Time is here."

She chuckled, a deep throaty sound. "It wouldn't be a White Cane event without Time." She adjusted her white cane, which was blue, to coordinate with her outfit, intent on leaving this group of volunteers for another.

Footsteps followed and fell with hers. "How about I walk with you?" a deeper, male voice suggested.

"Rodney? Is that you?"

"'Tis I," he said with a flourish. "I wanted to wait until you finished with your pictures.

"You could've photobombed us," she teased. She laid a hand on Rodney's arm; her tone was solemn. "I heard about

Winnie. I'm so sorry. And your company. Is there anything I can do?"

He patted her hand. "You're kind to offer," his voice held a catch. The ensuing swallow was loud. "I can't believe everything is gone. She ruined me."

"What's going to happen to your business and all the employees?"

"You sound just like my daughter." He laughed. "You both make me sound like a Fortune 500."

"How is Candace taking all of this?" Geneva had the impression of a shrug rather than actually seeing one as Rodney's muscle bunched beneath her palm.

"She's not happy about what's happening. Her biggest gripe is not being able to see me on a daily basis. And since her mother decided to move a hundred miles away, I don't get to see her at all. Not with her busy schedule."

"She's what, 16 and involved in the Robotics Club?"

"Wow. You have been listening." Surprise colored his voice.

Geneva laughed. "I try to listen and take in everyone's life. You're all so fascinating."

"Yes, we are a fascinating bunch. Fortunately, there is time to discuss my issues another day." He nudged her forward, and they resumed walking. "Today is a beautiful day. Not too hot with just the right amount of breeze to keep us all cool."

Geneva nodded. She was certain Rodney's voice held a tinge of bitterness and anger but let it go. He was right. There would be time to discuss his personal life, and today was a beautiful day.

She swung her cane back and forth with practiced ease. The smooth, plastic ball on the other end first moved over grass, then pebbles, and finally concrete. Lots of fun, laughter, and music filled the air. She breathed deep, inhaling the scent of grilled meat, hot buttered popcorn, and the sweet fragrance of spun sugar.

The annual White Cane event aimed to inform, educate, and empower the sighted world and anyone with blindness or visual impairment.

National White Cane Safety Day was still a few months away, but this gathering was a great way to get the community involved before the big day. Based on the buildup of noise, vendors showcasing available technology were bringing in quite a crowd.

The highlight of this event was to instill empathy into sighted friends and families by sharing what it was like to navigate a sighted world with limited to no vision.

"I hope they don't have some stupid reporter here who says how scary it is to cross the street," Rodney groused.

"It's like those trust-building exercises," Geneva began. "The ones where you fall backward and hope someone catches you."

"So, you agree with them going on air saying how scary it is."

"For them, it is. We're used to crossing streets, cooking, running with scissors, with no vision."

"Running with scissors?" He laughed.

A smile played at the corners of her mouth. "What? You don't?"

"Not recently."

"And then there's our friends with dogs who assist them across the street. Most reporters, heck, most sighted people find it scary how we rely on a dog to get us from point A to B."

"Don't forget the guide pony."

"I heard about that. Wouldn't that make a great article for the blog?"

"I hear Geneva and Rodney," a cheerful, female voice sang out.

"Abigail. You're as beautiful as ever." Rodney greeted Abigail with a hug. "And your guide is looking well too."

Abigail beamed, patting the head of her guide, Percy. "He's good. Pretty excited to show off today."

"Let me get a picture of the two of you," Geneva suggested.

"Of course."

Geneva fumbled in her pocket for her phone. She tilted left and right before she snapped several more pics.

"So, is everyone coming back to my place after we're done here?" Abigail asked. "The hall is set up for everyone."

"The division isn't holding it at their facilities?" Geneva couldn't keep the surprise from her voice.

"I managed to persuade them to have it at my place. Besides, the food and drinks are way better." Abigail grinned. She was the proud owner of Abigail's, a local bar and eatery.

"I'll say," Rodney added. "Where's the rest of our group?"

"Amelia and her husband are leading a sighted group through an obstacle course. Penelope is helping a group cross the street, and Time is in the dunk tank," Abigail answered. "And everyone else is milling around."

"Great. I'm going to wander a bit and grab some more photos before I have to meet my hubby so we can do another live video." Geneva snapped photos at random while she walked.

She loved events like these, and promoting awareness of what a white cane meant brought her a sense of empowerment.

Most sighted individuals could go their entire lives without ever meeting a blind person. Or the extent of their knowledge was of people like Annie Sullivan, Helen Keller, Stevie Wonder, or Ray Charles. But to interact with a blind or visually impaired person often seemed alien to them.

It seemed the world had protocols for translators and interpreters, but when it came to blindness, some rational people were at a loss. Visits to a doctor or other health care providers, if not forewarned, could produce meltdowns in an otherwise intelligent person. Just how hard was it to read out loud to someone without sight? These were just some of the challenges Geneva, and others, faced every day—which was where her blog came in.

She loved showing the world there were no limits on her other than what she placed on herself.

She did everything she wanted and felt no lack of contentment. A happy baby giggle split the air, and she smiled.

Well, there was one thing. Geneva paused. There was one thing that scared her—raising a child. It wasn't a matter of how to do it, but whether others would allow her and her visually impaired husband to raise a child.

She knew how to change diapers, prepare bottles, and such. After all, she spent many of her teenage years babysitting relatives and children in the neighborhood. She loved kids. But there were horror stories out there of Child Protective Services removing children from blind parents. Not because the parents were negligent or abusive, but because they couldn't see.

Geneva couldn't go through something like that. Not when she struggled and worked twice as hard just to get to where she was now.

A smattering of laughter broke her reverie. She shook off her momentary despair. Over pebbles and soft grass, finally to the solid concrete of the sidewalk, she followed the sound. The crunch of tires on asphalt and the occasional thud and bump of a vehicle hitting a pothole added to the noise.

The slap and thud of footfalls had her stepping closer to the edge of the sidewalk.

"Geneva?" an unfamiliar voice called.

She stopped and turned in the direction of the newcomer.

"It is you!" the younger but still unfamiliar voice exclaimed. "Oh my! This is such an honor. Could I have your autograph?"

Paper rattled. Geneva held out her hand in anticipation of the pen and paper. She had her signature guide as well.

"Honey, she's blind. She can't sign that," an older female voice, presumably the mother or some other guardianlike figure, admonished.

"Actually, I can." Geneva carefully spelled her name. She knew some who used a mark or symbol as their signature, but she knew how to write her name, which was a source of pride.

"Yeah, mom. Blind doesn't mean stupid," the younger voice explained. "Geneva says so all the time. You should see some of the things she and her friends can do."

"Oh. I'm sorry," the mom sputtered with embarrassment. "I didn't mean."

"It's okay," Geneva said with a chuckle. "I also take pictures, travel, shop, swim, and do just about everything I want."

"But you can't see," the woman blurted.

"Mother. You're embarrassing me," the teen cried in an aggrieved tone. "C'mon, Mom. Let's do the obstacle course. They blindfold you and time you to see how fast you can do it."

Geneva shook her head. The teen was informed, which was nice, but the mother typified what Geneva faced. Geneva giggled. Hopefully, after going through the obstacle course, both mother and daughter would better appreciate their sight and what it was like to be blind.

The day pretty much went on like that.

Geneva wouldn't consider herself a celebrity, but she did enjoy giving motivational talks and producing content for her website. She tilted her head to the side, listening for any clicks or other indication that her husband, Jethro, was on his way to her. She felt for the hands on her watch. A few more minutes remained before they went live. She could still take pictures.

A burst of laughter pulled her attention back to the group she heard before the teen and mom waylaid her. She moved in that direction.

The group of voices grew louder, and she paused to orient herself so she could capture as much of the street and group as possible. She propped her cane against the crook of her arm, its slight weight comforting as she raised her phone.

"My eyes! My eyes!" someone screamed. Geneva had trouble deciphering whether the voice contorted with pain was male or female.

She swung in the direction of the voice, her thumb flicking her phone screen. The rapid click of the shutter alerted her that her phone was taking multiple shots.

Tires on pavement skidded while brakes screamed and horns blared. A sickening thud and crunch made the world go still.

For the space of a heartbeat, silence hung before the street erupted in noise.

Mr. VIP smiled at the crumpled body in the street and the three smashed vehicles—his handiwork. *The only thing that would've made things better is if the stupid woman hadn't screamed about her eyes before I shoved her in the street.* Helping her into the road had been easy. He'd been with the group crossing the road. *It was nothing to give the irritating woman a little hip bump into oncoming traffic.*

Glancing around, he frowned. People held their phones high, trying to capture the scene. He wasn't worried about them; they were regular gawkers. He turned in a slow circle. Only one camera pointed in his direction. But two people were facing him.

He fixed his mind on the petite, dark-haired woman. Through her gray-tinted sunglasses, she seemed to stare right at him. *No. Not her. Anybody but her.* And there was another taller, dark-haired woman.

Had they seen him? Did they know what he'd done?

With growing apprehension, he watched as the petite woman pocketed her phone, and the two women embraced. There was no way they hadn't seen him and what he'd done. He couldn't allow that. It wasn't time for anyone to know who he was.

A tall, gangly black man with an even taller afro hurried and draped an arm around the petite woman's shoulders. He steered her toward the rest of the group huddled beneath the banner heralding "White Cane Awareness."

The taller woman held out a hand as if to stop the couple but whipped out a phone instead. She held it up. She turned and locked eyes with Mr. VIP.

Even from a distance, he heard the click of the camera shutter.

No. Mr. VIP turned to avoid the camera but was certain the woman had captured his face. If she did, he would eliminate her. If she didn't, well, he might let her live.

But he couldn't eliminate her. She'd been kind and seen him during his suffering. And yet, he couldn't share his secret with her. Not when she reminded him of the daughter he no longer saw.

Doubt lingered. Maybe, if he had to, he would make her death painless.

Chapter Two

Geneva shuffled the goodie bags and the mail as she waited for Jethro to unlock the door. After the accident, there wasn't much reason to stick around. And after all the socializing with strangers, she was drained.

"Sometimes I forget how popular my wife is," Jethro teased, relieving her of her packages. He held the door as she entered and locked it.

"Oh, stop," she giggled. "I love meeting new people."

A faint thud resounded on the hall table to her left. "Mail and bags are on the table. Why don't you tackle that while I get dinner?"

"I don't think I can eat," she called after him. "Could use some wine, though."

'It's only salad, and it will go great with the wine."

"Mm-hmm," she muttered as she moved to the table.

She sorted through the bags and their usual assortment of reusable drink bottles and pens. She felt several brochures in Braille and something squishy that might be a stress ball. She paused, skimming her fingertips over a small padded envelope.

She looked through the second bag and set it aside. It had all the same items except for the padded envelope. Next, she went through the mail, using an app on her phone to read through the assortment of junk mail, bills, and a few bulkier envelopes that felt like they contained discs.

With the mail in hand, she crossed over hardwood floors. Her footsteps echoed off the vaulted ceilings. She skirted the cushy leather sofa, rounded the accent table nestled behind it, and followed straight through the open door of the office she shared with her husband. There, her footsteps sank into plush carpeting. She wiggled her toes, grateful to be out of her sandals. She deposited the bulkier envelopes into a wire basket on Jethro's desk. She had a similar basket on her desk but seldom used it. She preferred to have her mail stacked on the center blotter. That way, what wasn't relevant could be immediately shredded and thrown away.

Clatters and thumps rolled from the kitchen. Jethro was never quiet when he did anything in the kitchen.

She put away the picnic souvenirs. Once the last water bottle found a home, she washed her hands and sat at the table. She skimmed a hand over the cool surface. Jethro already set out placemats, utensils, and napkins.

Footsteps shuffled on the hardwood before a plate clunked down in front of her. She heard another sound to her left. A quieter clink sent vibrations through her fingertips.

"I've set your wine next to your right hand," Jethro stated.

Geneva slid her fingers along the smooth surface of the table until she felt the cool stem of the goblet. She picked it up and moved it to the left side of her plate. She waited until she heard the scrape of the chair before she settled her napkin in her lap.

"I take it since you're drinking wine, the test was negative?" Jethro asked quietly.

"Jethro," she sighed.

He covered her hand with his. "It's okay, Geneva."

"No. It's not." She turned her hand and pressed her palm to his. "We're not normal. We wouldn't be normal parents. How will we know if our child is choking? Or has put something in its mouth or homework?"

"We've talked about this, Geneva."

She didn't like the patient humor infusing his voice.

"My dad raised me, and he's blind." He squeezed her hand. "We would use bells and baby-proof the house just like any other parent does when their infant becomes mobile. We'd teach our little one to speak instead of nod or shake its head."

"What if someone tries to take our baby from us?" Having a child taken away was the true root of her fear. "Like they did that one couple."

"Geneva, we have a great support system."

"So did that couple," she countered.

"They also had an ignorant nurse and incompetent medical staff. Our doctors and nurses know us. They're familiar with our needs. And when it comes time for the next step, we'll make the rounds of the nurses and doctors. We will meet the medical staff so they will be aware of our needs. And let's not forget we've got Murphy Giles as an advocate." A smile lit his voice. "Can you see anyone going against him? I swear people tremble when they hear his name."

Grudgingly, Geneva chuckled. "He can be pretty formidable."

Murphy Giles, a fellow member of the Council for the Blind, advocated as much as possible. He was instrumental in sweeping changes for local transportation and making things easier for visually impaired people to navigate airports and fly with their guide dogs.

"As quiet as it's kept, our chapter of the council assisted that couple as well as two other mothers keep their children."

She gripped his fingers. "Really?"

"We can do this, Geneva. For better or worse, we are in this together."

"But you still have some vision," she pointed out. Was that envy she heard in her voice? Was that another reason she was hesitant? That he would get to see some form of their baby that she never would?

Silence met her declaration.

"Jethro, I'm sorry." She loved her husband more than anything else in the world, and shame filled her as she realized the cruel, callousness of her words.

"It's understandable," he said, briefly squeezing her fingers.

His compassion made her feel more like a heel.

"I don't know what it's like never to see anything at all. Or wanting to see someone's face of whom you love." He released her hand to stroke her cheek. "What I do know is I love you and want to have children with you. I will describe what they look like, but you will be able to feel their little faces and toes and fingers. I know touch doesn't replace sight, but love transcends all of that."

"I don't deserve you." She swallowed the tears coating her throat.

"Which is why we're perfect for each other. I don't deserve you either, but I'm keeping you."

They fell into silence as they ate.

"I'm really glad you weren't crossing the street today," Jethro began. "You had me worried for a minute."

"I think we were all worried." Geneva sipped her wine, thankful for the topic change.

"I hope I wasn't too rude to your new fan."

"I seriously doubt that. I think that fan was more interested in the accident than you stealing me away." She exchanged her wine for more salad. "Did they find out who got hurt?"

"Sherry something or other. One of the volunteers said she owns a catering company."

"Sherry's Catering?" Geneva exclaimed. "S is for food?"

"Yeah. That's it."

"Oh, that's so tragic." She sipped more wine. "Was she one of the volunteers?"

Clothing rustled, and Geneva figured Jethro had shrugged.

"I think she was just looking." Utensils clinked on china. "I'm just glad it wasn't one of us or the volunteers."

"So, what happened?"

Chewing and swallowing were her answers for the moment. Instead of using her fork, she used her fingers to pick at the salad greens on her plate.

"From what I could gather, people say she ran into traffic. One driver swerved, but another hit her and another car."

Geneva nibbled on her chicken.

Jethro continued, "Someone even said she was pushed."

"Really? Why would anyone say that? Or even hint at something so awful?"

"Who knows. Can you imagine if any of us had been hit?" He covered her hand with his. "The Division would be swimming in lawyers and every other legal means to cover their behinds from any liability."

Geneva sat back. "Maybe we can send flowers or something. Her company did cater a few of the social events. And I think she may have been a friend of Murphy's. You know how he knows everybody."

"There's a last-minute get-together at Abigail's tomorrow night. Many of the group are shook, and they want to talk it out."

"At her home or the bar?"

"The bar. I don't think she wants a bunch of rowdy blind people at her house."

Geneva laughed, unsure if it was the laughter or the warmth of the wine relaxing her. After they finished eating in silence, Geneva cleared the dishes and loaded the dishwasher.

"Do you plan on working anymore tonight?"

"I need to return a few emails. Other than that, I'm yours."

"I put your mail in the basket," she called after him.

"You're a treasure," he returned.

Grinning, Geneva wiped down the counters using overlapping swipes to ensure she covered the entire surface. Once done, she started the dishwasher, then swept the floor using the same overlapping motion she'd used on the counters.

Above the K-Pop drifting from their home office, a synthesized voice spoke as keys clicked and clacked.

Geneva was proud of her husband. Not only did he teach classes in technology, but he specialized in assisting the elderly and visually impaired with how to improve their use of computers and other mobile devices.

She'd been blind since birth. Some complicated disease that had her born without eyes. But she enjoyed her world and never felt like she was missing anything—until she met Jethro. She adored her husband. And for once in her life, she wished she could see his handsome face.

Jethro considered himself legally blind. He had special glasses, which included a magnifying bifocal lens. He could only see with those glasses on. He used a cane the same as she, but often he went without one, preferring to use echolocation when he was out. She'd tried echolocation—making clicks by mouth to judge the distance of objects by the way the sound bounced back—but couldn't quite get the hang of it. She preferred her cane.

She paused as she replayed their earlier conversation. They'd been married going on five years, and they were both established in their careers in Ann Arbor, MI. Jethro was the head of technology for the elderly and disabled at the local vocational training school. She worked from home with blogs, websites, and podcasts. And the only thing missing from their lives was a baby. If they planned it, could they really raise a child?

They could do it. Both had family in the area and were active members of the Council for the Blind. Plus, there were plenty of parents in their group who had raised kids.

Rodney had a daughter.

She bit her lip. Maybe that wasn't a good example since his wife used his vision as a reason to block him from seeing his daughter. But Abigail, Time, and Murphy all raised children. They would be good resources. And like Jethro said, his father raised him.

Then there was another issue. What if their child was born blind? Did they have the right to bring another life into the world, knowing that child could be born with a disability?

No. Geneva shook her head. *I'm overthinking.* Both her parents had 20/20 vision, and she was born without eyes. She and Jethro had a good chance of producing a normal, healthy baby. And an equally good chance of producing a blind baby.

Geneva stood straighter. No matter what, she wouldn't let fear rule her decision. She wanted to be a mom and she was going to be the best mom possible. If she ever got the chance.

Chores complete, she grabbed her laptop and uploaded the pictures she'd taken. It would take her a little time to go through the ones she wanted to post on her website, but she could get them all on the computer in the meantime.

While the photos were uploading, she checked her email, pausing as a subject line caught her attention.

[Subject line: I want you.]

Thinking it was a love note from her husband, she selected the message and opened it. He often left her messages like that.

[Email: You're beauty is beyond measure and you smell so sweet. Seeing you today maid my heart beat. One day soon; I'll get you alone when I can. That's the only way to show you that I'm yo're biggest fan.]

Definitely not from her husband. Not with the obvious grammatical errors. Not that she was perfect, but she knew enough that "you're" was a contraction of "you are" and not the possessive 'your' the writer intended. Even "maid," a noun, was not the verb "made."

She sent the email to the trash. Just another crackpot email from a "fan" with too much time and Internet on their hands. She didn't see emails like that most of the time, but now and then, one leaked through.

Thinking better of it, she clicked on the trash icon, brought the message up again, and hit print. She also captured a screenshot. She sent the screenshot to a folder marked "The Looney File." The hard copy she would place in a similar file in her desk. *It never hurts to have a paper trail*.

Stifling a yawn, she closed the laptop lid. Mobile devices in hand, she entered the office. The K-Pop was louder. Hearing her footfalls, Jethro lowered the volume.

"Everything okay?" he asked, removing his headset.

"Yeah." Carefully, she set down the laptop and plugged it in. She set her phone on the charger. She then walked to Jethro and placed her hands on his shoulders. His muscles were firm but relaxed.

"How do you do that?" she asked in wonder. "I take one picture, and my shoulders knot up. You sit at the desk for an hour, and you're so loose."

He grasped her hand, brushing a kiss along the sensitive skin on the inside of her wrist. A shiver warmed her body.

"Maybe because it annoys you," he teased.

She laughed, using her free hand to caress his afro. She loved his hair, kinky and full. She leaned closer, inhaling the tropical scent of coconut and pineapple of his shampoo. His hair was soft despite its lamb's wool appearance. It had so much more character than her long, shoulder-length tresses.

For goodness' sake, her hair wouldn't even hold a curl, no matter how much hair spray and gel she used. Now, she flicked her straight hair over her shoulder as she dipped her hands beneath Jethro's shirt.

His skin was warm to the touch. His coarse hair met one of her palms as the other drifted over his chest and down his flat stomach.

"You're not playing fair." He kissed the inside of her elbow.

"It's been a long day, and I haven't had dessert."

The chuckle vibrated through her hands. "So, I'm your dessert?"

She kissed his jawline, just before his ear, knowing that was one of his sweet spots.

She was rewarded with a low moan.

"You don't play fair." He dragged her into his lap, kissing her lips, eyelids and finally settling on her mouth again.

She loved his mouth, so firm and commanding. She could lose herself in his kisses. The raw hunger she'd ignited conveyed itself in every press of his lips, in every nibble of his teeth and flick of his tongue.

She made a wholly feminine sound in the back of her throat. She threaded her hands through his hair, holding him in place while their tongues dueled.

Jethro stood. Geneva wrapped her legs around his waist. He settled her on a free area of the desk.

"We haven't used this room in a while," she whispered as she nibbled his ear.

He peeled off her sundress and kissed her shoulder as he slid off her bra strap.

She tilted her head to give him better access. There was nothing like being undressed by the man she loved. There was no hurry, only a sensuous slide of skin on skin. No matter how often they came together, it was always a giving and taking of love—an appreciation and exclamation that required physical touch.

He entered her, drawing a low, slow gasp of need from her lips. She pressed her mouth to his damp chest. He tasted of man and sweat. She reveled in him, enjoying the way their bodies clung to and grasped at one another in their lovemaking.

Geneva's orgasm crested and coasted over her and coaxed Jethro into his own. Jethro

dropped his head to her damp shoulder. He held Geneva close as he collapsed, with a satisfied sigh, into a nearby chair.

"I love that desk."

She giggled. "Me too."

Their pants rivaled the techno music now playing. Geneva curled into Jethro, rubbing her cheek against the coarse chest hair. "You always make me feel so good."

He kissed the top of her head. "You take my breath away. Maybe we can have a repeat in the bedroom?"

Geneva pressed a palm over his heart. "Maybe I'm too tired."

He stood, tossing her over his shoulder. She let out a squeal.

"We'll see about that."

⁓

Serefina stared at the ranch-style home. She was still buzzing from her meet and greet with Geneva. Serefina only followed Geneva to find out where she lived.

She approved of the one-story house—the cream brick contrasted nicely with the royal blue trim and doors. Red mulch that looked fresh surrounded the few decorative shrubs. She bent down, sifting a handful of the wood through her fingers. *Definitely fresh*. The scent of cut wood was strong. Tossing the chips back on the pile, she rose.

She darted carefully from shadow to shadow. All the time, she wondered if Geneva had received her poem. She was surprised at how well-kept the lawn was. The grass was thick and cushioned her footfalls. It was like walking on air, and she wondered if this was a deliberate thing because textures were important.

She knelt, caressing the grass. She crawled a few feet on hands and knees. Not a single rock, twig, or weed was in the vicinity. She stretched out, staring up at the stars. *Has Geneva done this very same thing, sans studying the stars part? Does Geneva lie in the grass and feel the earth's heartbeat? Does she press her fingers into the dirt and inhale the sweet fragrance of green? What a fabulous life Geneva lives.*

Pretending she had no sight, Serefina closed her eyes and listened to the night.

Sound carried—even in this quiet neighborhood. A car door slammed, and Serefina could hear, actually hear the tick of the cooling engine. Muffled voices drifted on the wind, as did the pungent burnt rubber, skunk scent of weed.

She wrinkled her nose in disgust. *Edibles are much better*. She appreciated the longer-lasting high and that she did not have to contend with her clothes and hair revealing what she had been doing.

An insect whined nearby, reminding Serefina of an old folktale about a mosquito. Something about the insect not warning before it bit. And every time it got close enough to a human to ask for forgiveness, the mosquito was slapped to death.

A motorcycle broke the stillness of the night, and Serefina marveled at the rumble and faint vibrations she felt.

Another car rolled by; its bass was loud enough to rattle the window panes.

She felt it. Really felt it.

These sensations had to be what Geneva felt, what she lived every day of her life. Serefina sat upright, pushing a strand of hair from her face. Excitement oozed through her. She opened her eyes. After her deliberate attempt at blindness, the orange glow of streetlights was overly bright. The momentary heightening of her other senses seemed to fade.

She scrambled to her feet. She had to know what the inside of the house looked like. Would it be like everyone else's house, or would there be something special that only Geneva would or could use?

Using the shadows, she moved closer to the house. As soon as she set foot on the first paving stone of the walkway, a light snapped on.

Blinded by the sudden brightness, Serefina gasped, shielded her eyes, and stumbled back to the shadows. Her heart was hammering so loud it was the only thing she could hear. She crouched in one of the few remaining shadows and counted. After five minutes, the light went out, and the night plunged into blessed darkness.

Lesson learned. She quickly walked down the driveway, up the block, and around the corner. She had to get in to see how Geneva lived. She glanced over her shoulder once or twice, making sure her footsteps didn't scuff or scrape the concrete. She could be stealthy when she wanted to.

The bright light was just a minor setback. Serefina hadn't known about it. After all, how could she? There wasn't anything online about Geneva's house. Serefina knew where Geneva lived because she followed the paratransit bus, which took Geneva and Jethro home.

Now that Serefina knew the house was on a cul-de-sac and that it had a motion-triggered floodlight, she could counter the light and not park in the in front of the house. She could use those things.

When she reached the corner, she turned. Staring through the yards, she could make out the rooftop of the cream and blue brick house. She would visit the house in daylight.

Quietly she entered her vehicle, glad it had an electric motor. Yes, she would come back during the day and see how Geneva lived.

Chapter Three

The next afternoon Geneva sat in front of her laptop, fingers flying across the keys. The voice announcing the letters as she typed spoke too fast. She smiled as she created the article to go with the pictures and videos she'd taken yesterday.

She paused. There was still a bunch of photos to go through from the previous day. And she couldn't help but think of the poor woman who'd lost her life. Rubbing her temples, she leaned back in her chair. Sherry wasn't the first small business owner to die. Geneva forgot about the article and did a quick search. She found dozens of articles on how to start a small business. After finessing her keywords, she finally found the stories. *Interesting*. Two owners, one of an A/V company and one of a companion care company, had died. At that moment, the police had no leads. There was also some vandalism on a few of the downtown properties. The offenses weren't enough to stop business, but they were enough to inconvenience the shop owners for a day or two.

Geneva reached for her phone and dialed Penelope. Someone answered after three rings.

"PB&J Bakery," a male voice greeted.

"May I speak with Penelope, please? Tell her it's Geneva."

"Hey, Geneva. It's Avery. She'll be glad to hear from ya. Hold a sec."

Avery placed her on hold, and a moment later, a breathless feminine voice filled her ear. "What's up, Geneva?"

"Is this a bad time?"

Penelope laughed. "Not at all. Your call gives me an excuse to get off my feet a moment. We've been swamped the last few days."

Geneva smiled. Penelope's bakery made her wedding cake a few years back. "I hope you don't mind my asking, but I'm calling about your shop being vandalized."

"Oh, that?" The sound of papers crinkling came through the line. "Sam was responsible for breaking my windows."

"Are you sure?"

"Of course. Sam and his group wanted to buy up the businesses around here and sell to some commercial dealer. The only thing is they couldn't get enough of the owners to sell to make the deal profitable. Once folks found out he was using less than legal tactics to strong-arm owners, the commercial deal fell apart." Penelope let out a heavy sigh. "This all happened around Valentine's Day. We were nearly overwhelmed with orders."

"Has anything happened since then?"

Something banged and buzzed in the background.

"Like what?" Penelope asked.

"Any other mishaps around your bakery or any of the other businesses near you?"

"Hold on, okay?"

Geneva waited as the phone clattered against a hard surface. Muffled voices drifted through the line, followed by laughter and a door slam.

"Sorry about that. Had a last-minute delivery. What were we talking about? Oh yes. The guy who put in the bakery's sound system was murdered. I think his son took over the business."

"Really?"

"Yeah. They're a few doors down from me. Real nice kid. He let me feel his locs. Nice, soft, and long." Penelope chuckled.

"Maybe I'm still a little jumpy from yesterday."

"I know, right? Avery was beside himself when it happened. I'd just finished leading a group of people across the street when it happened."

"None of the blind were hurt." Geneva pushed a strand of hair behind her ear.

"That's cause we know how to listen for traffic and wait on the curb to make sure nothing is coming," she said wryly. "We don't even dawdle in the middle of the crosswalk."

"Dawdle?"

"I had to prod two of them to keep moving. They kept looking at their phones."

"And how did you know they were looking at their phones?" she teased.

"They made little click sounds and kept commenting on what so and so said about what some guy was wearing. It freaked them out too when I told them to get off their phones and get out the street."

The doorbell pealed. "That's the door. Gotta go."

"Later."

Smiling, Geneva set down her phone and stood. "Who is it?" she called.

"It's Time."

Interesting. Geneva wondered why he was dropping by. Had she forgotten an appointment?

"What a pleasant surprise," she stated, opening the door. "What brings you to my neck of the woods?"

Swift Time, an older man with more salt than pepper hair, stepped across the threshold. He closed and locked the door. "I was wondering if you had a chance to recommend a reader."

"Really? You could've phoned me instead of dropping by."

"I had to make sure you were all right." His voice contained a smile but also held a faint note of tension.

Geneva made her way to the kitchen, where she put the kettle on for tea. While the water heated, she placed cookies on a plate. She set the plate on the eat-in counter along with mugs, a sugar bowl, and a small container of cream.

"You really don't need to go to such trouble."

"It's no trouble at all. Besides, I could use the sugar rush."

Wood scraped against the tile as Time settled in on a padded stool.

"I did want to make sure you were all right," he began. He selected a fig bar from the plate.

"That's right. You were there too. Did you see anything?"

"I was signing autographs," he mumbled around the cookie. He swallowed. "The police have asked for my assistance."

The kettle began its shrill shriek, and Geneva snatched it from the eye. Carefully, she poured the steaming liquid into two mugs already with teabags. She placed one in front of Time. "It's to the left of your plate."

"Thanks." He located the mug and poured a small bit of cream into the liquid before he removed the tea bag.

Geneva settled on a stool beside him. She spooned sugar into her tea. "Is consulting for the police something you do often?" she asked.

"I guess you can say they call me when something odd happens."

She tapped the plate and located one of the oatmeal raisin cookies. "What's so odd about yesterday's accident?"

"The woman screamed about her eyes before she was hit."

Geneva chewed, swallowed, and chased the crumbs with tea. "I do remember her saying that. It's what caught my attention."

Time nodded even though he knew Geneva couldn't see the gesture. "I told the police the same thing. No one really saw what happened. Or I should say all the statements are conflicting even the drivers can't really say what happened."

Geneva reached for a fig bar. "I called Penelope because she experienced some vandalism and such."

"I remember that. Actually, I think I was there the day she had to repair her door."

Geneva waited for him to say more. But after a lengthy silence, he didn't elaborate. "I'm fine. I was nowhere near the street when it happened."

Time heaved a sigh. "Forgive me if I scare you, Geneva, but I do hope you'll heed my words."

A shiver of unease trickled down her spine. She knew Time was a little eccentric, and sometimes he knew things before they happened. But after yesterday's events, she, at the very least, wanted to hear him out.

"Do you have a warning for me?" She kept her tone light.

"I know you don't put much stock in the things I see, but do an old man a favor and be careful."

She chuckled. "There is nothing old about you, Time."

He touched her hand. His palm was rough and calloused against the back of hers. "Please be careful."

"Of course."

Time stood. "Thank you for the tea and cookies."

Geneva slid off her stool and followed Time to the door. "Anytime."

"If you and your husband are free this evening, stop by the high school. I'm wrestling tonight."

She clapped her hands. "We'd love to. I'll let Jethro know."

Chapter Four

Excitement buzzed and bounced off the gymnasium ceiling. Geneva clutched Jethro's arm as she bounced in her seat. Around them, the crowd ebbed and flowed like a good tide.

"This is so amazing," she gushed. "Are any of the wrestlers out yet?"

"People are still coming in." Jethro pried Geneva's fingers from his arm. "Sit tight. Abigail and a few others just walked in." Jethro walked away, the sound of his tongue clicking lost in the sea of noise.

Smiling, Geneva raised her phone. She could capture random images. Whether they were centered was irrelevant. She wanted to capture the energy of the crowd.

Someone swept by her, nearly knocking her over. She staggered back into the chair, dropping her phone to the wooden floor.

"Hey!" She righted, then reached for her talking phone.

"Here ya go," a deep male voice said.

Geneva closed her fingers around the device.

"Are you okay?" the male voice asked.

"Yes." She silenced her phone and shoved it in her pocket. With the back of her hand, she brushed her long hair from her face. "Yeah. Thanks for getting my phone. Did you see the jerk who ran into me?"

"Some ill-mannered teenager."

She heard the smile in his voice. "Thanks."

"Are you here by yourself?"

A smile curved her lips. *Is this guy hitting on her?* "No. I'm here with my husband. He went to grab a friend."

The man moved closer. "You're very pretty. If you were my wife, I wouldn't let you leave my side."

It wasn't so much his nearness that made her smile falter; it was the undertone of his words. They were pleasant enough but off somehow. She stepped back, putting more space between them. She flinched as he touched her hair.

"You presume too much." She knocked his hand away.

Click-click. Geneva whirled at the sound and moved forward. Geneva didn't want to be away from Jethro a moment longer. Like most blind and visually impaired people, Geneva had more restricted personal space boundaries. The stranger had gone too far by touching her hair and trying to engage her in an unwelcomed tone.

"Geneva?" Jethro grasped her outstretched arm and pulled her to him. "Baby, what's wrong?"

"I—" She stopped, not sure what to say.

"You're trembling."

Am I? She clung to her husband a moment. "Someone ran into me and knocked my phone out my hand."

Jethro ran his hands up and down her arms.

Geneva drew in a stuttered breath. Maybe she had let what Time said to her earlier get to her. "Did you find Abigail?"

"He sure did," the other woman piped up. Amelia couldn't make it, but Joshua said he would come and give audio description for us."

Geneva allowed Jethro to lead her back to their seats. "Is Amelia all right?"

"She's fine," Joshua interjected. "She's entertaining Gage or rather being entertained by him and his tuba."

"Oh, I forgot he was back in town," said Geneva.

Jethro guided Geneva's hand to a chair, and she sat.

"I brought Murphy and Dana with me," said Joshua.

Everyone exchanged pleasantries as they settled into their seats.

"Are you okay?" Abigail asked, leaning closer to Geneva.

"I am. Where's Percy? I don't want to step on him by accident?"

Percy was Abigail's guide. An English Labrador. He was stockier and more muscular than his American counterpart.

"Settled beneath my chair like the champ he is," Abigail answered. "Have you seen Swift wrestle before?"

"Once or twice. The crowd loves him."

The announcer's deep melodious voice said, "Ladies and gentlemen!" And the wrestling began.

―

Serefina checked her phone. She tapped the little notification and a ten-second video filled the screen. How she'd have loved to be at the wrestling match with Geneva. The angle was a little off-center, but the restlessness and excitement of the crowd came through loud and clear.

"Just a teaser before the match begins," came Geneva's bright voice.

Serefina replayed the video three more times before she shoved the phone in her pocket. Now she focused on the house. In the daylight, she observed blooming marigolds, hollyhocks, and crocuses. There were more decorative shrubs and fragrant, red mulch. Serefina walked up the driveway as if she had every right to be there.

When she was there the previous night, she'd noticed an open window on the back of the house. She peered to her right; a privacy fence lined the lawn between Geneva's house and her neighbor's, to her left was the open field. Serefina had nothing to worry about from that end. And she didn't need to worry about the floodlight going off either.

She checked the window, removed the screen, and set it aside. She didn't want to damage it. With a grunt, she hoisted herself onto the sill and did a belly slide through the opening.

She barely missed a wooden shelf filled with crystal figurines. The thumb-sized crystal butterfly and mouse winked in the evening sun.

Fingers trembling, she reached for one of the larger pieces of quartz polished to a high shine. One side featured the etched image of the Arch in St. Louis and the name of the monument and museum. She replaced it.

She released a small squeal of excitement. She was in Geneva's gorgeous house.

The wood floors gleamed. There were decorative art pieces on the walls. Abstract watercolors that were just blobs of colors to her. A yarn basket stood near a chaise, and a mounted flat-screen sat across from a tiny sectional—*a cozy space to watch a movie.*

Serefina wandered to the basket, which housed a long, colorfully striped snake. She presumed it would be a variegated scarf when finished.

She wandered through the house. It was spotless. No throws or area rugs covered the wooden floors. *And what is that?* She sniffed the air. Cinnamon. She followed the scent to a carpeted room. She stood on the threshold, allowing her eyes to adjust to the sudden dimness.

Two L-shaped desks were facing one another—the long legs of the L stood against the outer walls.

She saw the colorful hair tie on the left desk and hoped it was Geneva's. She crossed the thick carpet, pausing just long enough to appreciate the plushness. Heart pounding, she sat in the leather chair.

The faint scent of plums and honey rose around her. Serefina closed her eyes, breathing in the aroma of perfection. She was sitting where Geneva sat. Wow. Now she had to see where Geneva slept.

Serefina left the office searching for the bedroom and found an additional bathroom, a guest bedroom, and a laundry room. She walked toward the last door and wiped her sweaty palms on her jeans. She twisted the knob and pushed the door open.

Soft blues and greens gave the space a calm, tropical feel. Serefina noticed the vibrant bedspread that picked up cool blues and greens and added a pop of coral.

The room was tidy. Not a single article of clothing littered the plush carpet.

A plain, simple box drew her attention to the dresser. Curious, she lifted the lid and gasped. Inside were four pairs of eyes, from hazel to toffee brown. Each pair was in a separate case. These were Geneva's prosthetic eyes. With reverence, she circled each orb with her fingers. Serefina then held the eyes to her face. *Maybe I can get contacts to change my eye color.* She returned the eyes to their cases. She hesitated as her hand hovered over the box. Everything in her wanted to take one. *Geneva actually had these eyes in her body.* Her fingers closed around the hazel set. But if she took them, Geneva would know they were missing. With a sigh, she let the eyes be.

She moved to the chest of drawers, opening one after the other, plunging her hands inside to feel the cotton and lace.

She picked up a pair of neatly folded bikini panties and brought them to her nose. They smelled faintly of plums and a wholly female scent. She spread them out on the surface of the dresser. They were a turquoise blue with strings of silver running through the lace. She looked in the drawer again and pulled out the matching bra. These she stuffed in her pocket.

Oh god. Oh god, oh god, oh god. Serefina was going through Geneva's underwear drawer. She made sure she didn't leave a mess, then went through Geneva's closet.

Geneva had so many pretty things. Serefina moaned and groaned as in orgasmic ecstasy.

Safety pins hung from some hangers, while others sported wooden beads like necklaces. Serefina pushed the hangers back and forth before realizing the pins and beads were a way of coordinating clothes. She hummed to herself as she thumbed through the dresses, pants, and tops.

Geneva had great taste. Serefina fingered a pale green peasant blouse and a coordinating print skirt. She remembered Geneva wearing that outfit a few weeks ago for a local news interview.

She rubbed her face against the cotton. She wanted to be Geneva, and she figured she could achieve that with Geneva's clothes. She carefully removed the outfit from the hangers and neatly folded each item. She couldn't shove the entire outfit in her pocket.

Serefina hoped Geneva wouldn't miss the outfit or any of the other items. *Geneva won't miss a bottle of perfume or a few pieces of jewelry.*

Serefina gathered her treasures and went back to the office. She hadn't thoroughly looked through Geneva's workspace. But now, she would. Serefina focused on a piece of paper on the printer. *Maybe it is something from her blog.*

Serefina snatched up the page, and her breath caught in her throat. She grabbed the desk for support. It was her poem.

Geneva had printed out her poem. Even though she couldn't see the words, she'd printed it out. Elated, Serefina looked for more evidence of her printed poetry. She rummaged through drawers and finally found a folder with more of her poems.

Tears streaked her cheeks, and she had to fight back a sob. *It is kismet. Geneva knows I am her biggest fan and even created a folder for my poems!*

A chime split the air, and Serefina jumped. She juggled her phone. It was another notification from Geneva. Serefina hurriedly gathered up her treasures. She needed to get out of there. It wouldn't do to have Geneva come home and find Serefina in residence before Serefina was ready.

Serefina shoved the folder back in the drawer. She wiped her face, made sure she left nothing behind, and exited the same way she entered. With the purloined clothes stuffed under her shirt and her pockets full of jewelry and other finds, Serefina returned the screen to its mooring.

Today has been a good day.

――

Mr. VIP leaned against the wall, oblivious to the people cheering or booing around him. Geneva hadn't reacted to him until he touched her hair. More importantly, she hadn't recognized him either. *Blind. The woman is totally and completely blind.*

There is no way she could've gotten a picture of me on her phone.

He studied her now. She was petite, and her dark-brown hair flowed around her shoulders. She held up her phone. He could just make out the screen as she snapped picture after picture. The shots were surprisingly centered and clear. *Maybe if I'd had more time with her phone?*

He shifted to keep her in his limited field of vision. She was jumping up and down.

"And the match you've all been waiting for. No holds barred with one fall. You're challenger, 'Dees Nuts." The crowd hissed and booed as a large, bald, black man strutted into the gym. He wore a scowl and cast a dismissive glare at anyone foolish enough to meet his gaze.

"And your champion, three-time stroke survivor, cancer survivor, and Michigan's own Miracle Man, Father Time!"

The gym erupted with loud cheers and whistles; the sound vibrated through Mr. VIP's chest.

Mr. VIP stood back and clenched his fist as he glared at Father Time being led into the gym by a curvy, black woman in a veil and blue scrubs.

How he despised Father Time. *The man is up there flaunting his disability and using his hardships to inspire. Inspire!*

Mr. VIP breathed deep, working to contain the rage and hatred roiling in his veins. Every cell of his body wanted to storm the ring and smack Father Time with a steel folding chair.

Thwack! The sound of flesh on flesh echoed off the rafters. Scoop. Slam. A heavy body hit the springy blue mat and rebounded.

"Father Time. Father Time," the crowd chanted.

He wanted to cover his ears. He wanted the crowd to chant his name, *not the name of some old man looking for pity and sympathy.*

A petite figure caught the edge of his vision. Once more, she waved her phone in the air. *I have to get rid of her.* But first, he would find out if she'd captured him on her phone.

If it were possible, the noise level increased. Mr. VIP shifted to see why. Time was climbing the ropes. Walking the top rope, he held his opponent's arm. Once he reached the middle, Father Time leaped, bringing an elbow to his opponent's shoulder.

Father Time rolled his opponent to his back and pinned him. A deafening roar filled the space as the referee counted to three.

"And the winner and still champion, Father Time!" the announcer intoned.

"There are three things you don't do," Father Time gasped into the mic. "You don't spit in the wind. You don't tug on Superman's cape. And you don't mess with Father Time."

Mr. VIP stomped away from the gym in disgust. As he made his way out of the school, he could still hear people chanting, "Mr. Tick Tock." Mr. VIP pulled out his cane. He hated the thing, but he didn't want to fall down the steps either. He carefully made his way to a waiting sedan.

"Did you enjoy the event, sir?" the driver asked.

"I did. Saw some friend of mine. They're dying to meet up with me again." He smiled at his little joke as his driver closed the door. *Yes, Indeed. His friends will die.*

"So, what really happened at the wrestling match?" Jethro demanded once he and Geneva were in bed.

"It's hard to explain, Jethro. The guy didn't threaten me, but he made me feel like he was threatening me." She nestled deeper into Jethro's arms, glad he was so much bigger than she.

"How so?"

"He was pleasant. Made a little joke about not leaving me alone if I were his wife, but it was the way he said it." She frowned, trying to recall the exact tone. "He sneered it, and then he touched my hair."

Jethro bristled beside her. "He put his hands on you?"

She laid a palm on his cheek, enjoying the scrape of his beard. "He only touched my hair."

"That was more than enough."

"What's really weird is he seemed familiar."

"Not him trying to touch your hair?" Jethro poked Geneva.

She squealed and wiggled away from his torturing fingers. "You're so juvenile."

He kissed the top of her head. "But you love me."

"I do, but I think he was testing my sight."

Jethro barked a laugh.

"Not funny."

"I always find it funny when people try to test to see that we're really blind or something. It's not like we go around faking it."

"Some people do," she pointed out.

"And those people are sick weirdos." He flopped to his back. "You know, if we had a choice in the matter, we wouldn't be blind, visually impaired, or any of the other things we label ourselves." He huffed. "If the sighted people only knew how hard it is to live in their world."

"Bad day at work?"

"There's this woman. She's got cataracts and can't see her hands in front of her face. She's complaining about how she can't see and how hard it is for her to navigate." He huffed again. "She's bitchin' and moanin' about not seeing, and all the time I want to yell at her that she has a curable condition. Some doctor can dilate her eyes, and twenty minutes later, she has a nice new, shiny lens. Whereas you and I will never see a rainbow or a frickin' picture without some type of aid."

She pressed a kiss to his biceps. It wasn't the first time he'd had this complaint. She'd had the same gripe as well, and it was an oft lament of theirs and their group. So many took their sight for granted when it could so easily disappear—whether in an accident, disease, or some other malady.

"I appreciate what sight you have," she told him after a while.

He kissed her lightly. "I didn't mean you."

"I know," she said with a laugh. "I think you're so amazing at what you've done and have accomplished."

"You're the amazing one. There are days I watch you and can't believe I had the good fortune to find someone so feisty and independent. The fact you're blind never even crossed my mind."

Geneva burst out laughing. "You are such a dork."

He laughed, rolling until he blanketed her body. "Let me show you how much of a dork I am."

Chapter Five

Water bubbled in a fountain, and a few leaves crunched and crinkled beneath heavy booted feet. A chill wind carried the scent of damp, burning leaves and stale alcohol.

Mr. VIP listened for any hint of sound. All he heard was his breathing. He carefully made his way from the small park to the locked backdoor of a local eatery and bar. His knit mask pulled at his face when he smiled.

This is going to be so much fun. Mr. VIP flexed his fingers inside his gloves. With practiced ease, he picked the lock. *Forget the new-school techs with the gadgets. Give me hands-on any day. Picking locks is all about touch anyway.*

Once inside, he deactivated the alarm. Maybe Abigail shouldn't have told him the passcode. He hesitated, debating on whether he should remove his ski mask. Even if he did, no one would believe he was doing this.

He walked through the bar.

He bumped into the furniture without care. If anything, he went out of his way to knock over tables and chairs. He found the noise the wood and metal made as it clattered to the floor to be cathartic. The therapy didn't stop there. He rounded the waist-high bar, rummaged beneath, and came up with a wooden bat.

Hefting the weight, Mr. VIP gave a practice swing. The bat hemmed through the air.

Lovely indeed. He pivoted and swung at the nearest shelf of booze.

"And it's good!" he shouted when glass and alcohol filled the air.

"Oh, Abigail." Geneva wrapped her friend in a fierce hug. Even with the overhead fans working double time and the open doors and windows, the heady scent of alcohol still provided a buzz.

Abigail swiped at her tears. "Came in this morning to find my place destroyed." She sniffled. "P-Percy wouldn't even let me walk into the foyer. There was so much debris."

They sat on a bench at the back of the building. It was a small covered patio where employees could take breaks.

"How did they get in?"

"The police are questioning everyone who has a code." Abigail absentmindedly scratched under her dog's chin. "I've been here for almost twenty years and have never had any trouble like this."

"This is so disturbing," Geneva muttered. "Wait. Did you say the police were questioning the employees?"

"Just those who had a code. Only management and a few trusted vendors have it."

"Surely one of them wouldn't do something like this," Geneva protested.

"No. None of my staff would do this."

The door squeaked open. Footsteps echoed on the concrete. "Is this your cane, Abigail?" an unfamiliar voice asked.

Out of habit, Geneva patted the bag she carried. The weight of her collapsible cane was inside. "I've got mine," Geneva announced.

"It's probably one of the extra ones I keep on hand, Kyle," Abigail answered.

"The insurance adjuster is almost finished. As soon as he's done, we'll start cleaning up," Kyle informed. "There's so much glass on the floor. I'm afraid the pooch might pick up a sliver."

"The concern is appreciated. Is there any other good news?"

"It was only the stock on the shelves. Backstock is untouched, as are the other glasses and such. Once we get everything cleaned, we can still open today."

"That is good news."

"Indeed," Geneva agreed.

"Oh. I also gave pertinent parties a copy of the security tape." With that, Kyle's footsteps receded, and the door squeaked open and slammed shut.

"Well, the cameras should help," Geneva said.

"We just had the system updated not too long ago. It's a real shame about the owner. He was killed around Valentine's Day."

"You used the same AV company as Penelope?"

"Yes. They have a very good grasp of what I needed, and Penelope suggested them when she learned I wanted to update my system."

The door squeaked open again. "Abigail. The insurance man needs your signature."

Abigail stood. Percy gained his feet with a stretch and a jangle of dog tags. "Duty calls."

Geneva hugged her friend again. "Good luck. We'll talk later."

As the door closed behind Abigail and her employee, Geneva made her way off the patio. Using her cane, she navigated the sidewalk around to the front of the building. She had plans to meet Jethro in the nearby park.

She pulled her jacket closed as a chill breeze whipped through her. Crinkling leaves cartwheeled across the sidewalk in front of her and she scattered the leaves with a combination of her cane and feet.

A smile touched her lips. Geneva and Jethro always picnicked in the park before it got too cold. With the sun shining, it would be a nice change of pace. She almost didn't register the footsteps scraping pavement behind her.

A sharp gasp drew her attention. Geneva turned, and something hard and heavy slammed into her.

She cried out as she fell to the ground. Her breath left in a whoosh as the wind was knocked from her.

The cane she held clattered on the sidewalk. Someone ripped her bag from her shoulder, and the sound of footsteps meant they ran away.

"Hey! Hey!" More footsteps thundered past.

Geneva gasped the air, waiting for her lungs to catch up with the rest of her body. Had she just been mugged?

"Are you okay?" Gentle hands touched her sleeve. "Are you hurt?"

She shook her head, still unable to speak.

"Let's get you off the ground." Those same gentle hands helped her stand, then led her to a nearby bench. "Did you see what happened?"

"No. I'm blind." She swiped at the tears on her face. "Someone knocked me down and snatched my purse."

"Brian!" Geneva still couldn't figure out if the speaker was male or female. "That guy mugged a blind woman."

Someone, presumably Brian, trotted up. "I found her bag," he panted. "I'm sorry. We didn't get a good look at him. Is there someone we can call for you?"

Clicking met her ears. "My husband. He's coming this way."

"I'll bring him," Brian offered. "What does he look like?"

At this, Geneva smiled. "Tall, with an afro. He's visually impaired."

Brian patted her hand, and his footsteps receded. "Oh, dear. You're bleeding."

Stinging pain sang from the wound on her knee and the heels of her hands. "Oh. Ow."

Footsteps thudding on the pavement reverberated through the soles of Geneva's shoes.

"Where is she?" came Jethro's frantic voice.

"Here." A fresh wave of tears slipped down her cheeks. "I'm here, Jethro." A moment later, her husband engulfed her in his strong arms.

He ran his hands over her, stopping to inspect her hands and the rip in her leggings. "It's only scrapes." He kissed her again. He held her close. "What happened?"

"We saw someone shove her down and run off with her bag," Brian said. "I retrieved the bag but was unable to catch the man."

"I've got some water here," the woman offered. "And some bandages." She knelt in front of Geneva and tended her wounds.

"Thank you both," Jethro said, his voice thick with emotion.

"I called the police on the way back," Brian said. "I thought."

"Geneva?" Jethro prodded.

"I have my bag back."

"Is anything missing?"

Someone placed the bag in her lap. She rummaged through the pockets. Frowning, she went through them again. Stylus, slate for making notes in Braille. Her wallet. She double-checked her cards and ID were still intact. Even the bit of money folded in various ways was still there.

"Well?" Jethro prompted.

"My phone. I don't have my phone."

Chapter Six

Serefina gasped. She couldn't believe what she'd witnessed. A man knocked Geneva to the ground and stole her purse. *How dare he!*

The only reason Serefina was at the park was to catch another glimpse of Geneva, and if the mood was right, maybe sit and chat with her. Serefina had safely hidden her pretty, stolen treasures from her drunk of a husband. Besides, as long as there were cold brews in the fridge, the man left her alone.

Serefina had been admiring Geneva's floral patterned leggings and ice blue tunic when she saw the man rush forward, shove Geneva down, and steal her bag.

She hesitated, hating to see her idol harmed. *But if I recover Geneva's purse, maybe that would endear me a little more?*

A man of average height ran after the purse while a woman in jeans and a Michigan sweatshirt knelt to assist Geneva. Serefina chased after the men.

She was just in time to watch the thief. The thief rummaged through the bag, then threw it aside. He pocketed something in his jacket and kept running.

The second man stopped when he saw the bag on the ground. Not seeing the thief, the second man walked back to the park. Serefina followed the thief.

She followed him a few blocks away to a coffee shop. He stood three spots ahead of her in line. Serefina grabbed a water from the cooler and thunked it on the counter when it was her turn. She pivoted to keep the man in sight.

He wore thick glasses and wasn't old, but he wasn't young either. And he seemed familiar. Serefina searched her brain for when or where she could've seen him, but nothing came.

She swiped her debit card and searched the area near the man for an open seat. There wasn't one, but there was a chair near the entryway where she could keep him in sight.

Serefina pretended to look at her phone while the man glanced around the room. He then pulled a phone from his pocket.

Anger surged through her, and she squeezed the water bottle. The plastic crinkled. He'd stolen Geneva's phone. *What could he possibly want with that?*

Mr. VIP knew he had a limited amount of time to find what he needed. If Geneva were as smart as he thought she was, she would either try to locate her phone using the find app or lock and wipe the phone's memory. Either way, he had to get to her photos and find out if his picture was on her phone.

He was well-versed in working around people's passwords. He was also smart enough not to take the phone back to where he lived. Instead, Mr. VIP opted for a coffee shop bustling with business people, harried moms looking for a caffeine fix, and a few others he couldn't quite identify.

As he worked on the phone, he mulled over how he'd gotten the device. He'd heard the man chasing him. Snatching Geneva's bag so close to the bar, where someone could see him, had been a risk. *But without risk, there could be no reward. I have to take a risk if I want to keep killing.*

He might not want to kill Geneva, but he'd do it if he had to. For now, he had to be content with knocking her down and stealing her purse. A smile creased his lips. He had enjoyed shoving the petite woman to the ground. *It served her right for being such a busybody.*

Sweat beaded on his brow. Time was ticking away, and he had to get to the pictures. Placing his index finger near the bottom of the screen, he held it there until the phone vibrated. Then, he swiped upward and saw various icons.

He blew out a breath. *Now, to get to the photos.* He tapped the photo album, appreciating the petite woman's organization. She had labeled all her albums and events. Even the few photos she'd taken today were in their own folder. He scrolled until he came to the White Cane Event. There were nearly three hundred photos.

As quickly as the phone allowed, he swiped through the album. He bypassed photos of volunteers, his fellow council members, and a good snapshot of the banner over their table. There were shots of cars, flowers, grass, and people walking back and forth across the street.

Okay, I am getting closer to the timeframe of the accident. He was in the middle of the group. He could just make out Penelope at the front.

The pictures seemed to go frame by frame. The walk sign was blazing its white pedestrian figure. There was a group stepping off the curb. The sign now flashed red with a thirty-second countdown. Two women paused in the middle of the road as the group separated.

Penelope ushered them forward. Two seconds remained on the walk sign as the group made it to the curb.

He swiped to the next photo, and the screen went blank. *"No!"*

[This phone is lost. If found, please call 734-555-9898.]

"Dammit!" He slammed the phone on the table. He'd taken too much time.

The device was useless to him now. Shoving away from the table, he stalked toward the exit. As he neared the doors, a woman with long brown hair gave him pause. His pulsed tripped triple time. *How did Geneva get there so fast?* The woman raised her head. Instead of the sunglasses he expected, the woman wore none. At least she had eyes—brown ones.

He allowed relief to wash over him even as a tingle of familiarity slid through him. It wasn't Geneva, but he'd seen the woman before.

He hurried from the coffee shop. Once outside, he dropped the phone on the cement and stomped out his frustration. He didn't bother to retrieve the mangled glass and plastic. Someone else could take care of that.

As Serefina followed the man out, he was sure he had recognized her. She'd seen a flicker of surprise and confusion as he hurried out. She stuffed her water in her bag before looking up and down the sidewalk. A spot of color on the otherwise drab street caught her attention.

As Serefina walked toward the spot of color, a sinking feeling roiled in her gut. A moan of anguish left her lips as she dropped to her knees. He'd broken Geneva's phone. *What type of savagery is this? First, he shoves Geneva down, and then he breaks her phone.* Carefully, Serefina picked up the remnants of the phone. She swept the smaller pieces onto a receipt using her hairbrush and stored the shards in a wadded napkin. She made sure not a scrap of glass or plastic remained. *If I had Geneva's phone, maybe I could find out why the man hurt my idol. Once I knew that information, then I could go to Geneva. Or maybe with Geneva's phone, I could become Geneva.*

By the time Geneva and Jethro made it home, Geneva was stiff, sore, and anxious from her ordeal. Since neither she nor her good samaritans could describe the man who'd attacked her, the police could do little more than file a report for her stolen phone. At least she could provide the insurance company with the complaint number.

"Our picnic was ruined," she complained, limping into the bedroom.

"After everything that's happened, that's what you're upset about?" Amusement lit Jethro's voice.

Geneva paused in stripping off her ruined clothes. "Yes." She dropped the soiled garments in the hamper. "Phones are replaceable. Time with my husband is not." She continued into the bathroom, where she wrenched the knobs on the shower to the 'on' position.

"Aw. You really do love me." He came to lean on the door jamb.

"It's the hair," she called over the water.

He laughed. "Enjoy your shower."

Geneva bit back a hiss as the warm water trickled over her abrasions. In a warped way, the water made her aches better. She sighed as she allowed the water to massage the tension from her body. She reached for the plum-scented body wash she favored and came up empty. She ran her fingers over each bottle. She felt the tall, rectangular shape of Jethro's body wash, another cylindrical bottle with a push cap, her shampoo's pump bottle, and a conditioner bottle with a rubber band and bead. Her squat, oval bottle of soap was not there.

"Hey, babe," she raised her voice to be heard over the water. "Did you move my soap?"

"Ah, no," came the response. "I can get you another if you like."

"Thanks." She swept her foot along the shower floor, making sure the bottle hadn't found its way there.

"Here ya go." Something tapped the glass shower door. She reached out, and Jethro slapped the bottle into her palm.

"I used it this morning," she muttered, squirting the fragrant liquid into her palm. "And it's not on the floor."

"Maybe it fell behind the other bottles," Jethro suggested. "I'll look for it when you get out."

"Or you could join me and wash my back."

"Very tempting offer, but I gotta feed you." He left the room whistling.

Geneva smiled. Her husband loved taking care of her.

When she finished, Geneva pat dried her cuts and applied new bandages. Music drifted from the other room.

"When you're dressed, come into the living room," Jethro called.

Geneva rummaged through a drawer for a nightshirt. Frowning, she stopped. Her underthings were jumbled and not as precise as they were this morning. She righted the clothes. *Well, maybe I mussed them when I got dressed. After all, I was in a hurry.* She searched each drawer for her satiny sleep shirt. When she couldn't find it, she settled on one of Jethro's t-shirts. The soft cotton drifted down her curves and brushed her knees. Satisfied with her clothing choice, she walked to the living room.

The earthy scent of leaves and spicy cinnamon filled the air.

"Stop right there," Jethro said.

Fabric rustled, and joints popped.

Geneva stifled a giggle. "I heard that."

"I felt it," he grimaced. "Sorry we couldn't have our customary picnic in the park. We'll have it in the living room." He led her around the sofa until their bare toes touched a rough blanket.

Burning tears fell from her eyes as she lowered to the floor. She felt along the blanket to a woven wicker picnic basket resting near the center.

"Oh, Jethro."

He lifted her hand and placed a plate in her palm. "Just some nibbles to get started. He sat next to her. "There's cheese cubes, grapes, a few strawberries."

She leaned her head on his shoulder. "Tell me. How was your day?"

"Much better than yesterday," he answered. "I'm putting together a proposal for another class on accessibility features for mobile devices."

Geneva popped a grape in her mouth. "Cool. You should let the Council know. Some of them would enjoy knowing how to use their phones better."

He lifted her legs and set them in his lap. He proceeded to rub her feet.

"That feels exquisite."

They fell in companionable silence.

"You haven't touched your wine," Jethro pointed out.

She leaned forward, caressing his cheek. "We're going to have fun trying to make a baby."

A few afternoons later, Geneva and her assistant, Caitlin, sat at the dining room table. Geneva's new phone sat half in and out of its box next to her open laptop.

"You're the only one I know of who keeps her devices updated and backup almost to the minute," Caitlin commented. "It makes things so much easier."

"You're telling me," Geneva said with a sigh. "I'd be mortified if I'd lost all the pictures I've taken over the last week."

Caitlin clicked the mouse. "Yes, indeed." The mouse scrolled, and a faint sound like a playing card in bicycle spokes filled the silence. "You've got some really great shots."

"I need to add the ones of two or three different groups crossing the street. Penelope and Avery at the table, and Amelia and Joshua doing their self-defense demonstration."

As she spoke, Caitlin clicked, dragged, and dropped.

Clicking stopped. "Who's this?" Caitlin asked. "The two of you could be sisters."

"Who is who?"

Caitlin chuckled. "Your pictures are so good I forget you can't see. A young lady grinning broadly with her arm around your shoulder. I'm presuming she's a fan. There's another pic of you signing an autograph."

Geneva sat back with a ghost of a smile on her lips. "She was really sweet. I told her I'd put her pic on the website. She had no problem signing the waiver either." A phone chimed, and the accompanying vibrations shook the table.

"It looks like you got another with her just before the accident." Caitlin resumed typing.

"It was a busy day, and you know how I don't like to say no to my fans."

"Goodness. I heard about what happened to Abigail's place. Who would do such a thing?"

"I've no idea."

"And you're okay?"

"Of course."

"Jethro mentioned you were mugged." The clicking stopped. "Nothing like that ever happens."

A male voice announced the time on Geneva's phone. She picked up the phone and scrolled through her messages. The speed at which the voice spoke seemed too fast, but Geneva caught every word. She dictated a text. She listened to a few more messages and stopped, not sure if she'd heard it right.

[You're home is my home. I walked inside. You like my poetry I was so happy I cried. It excites me knowing I can, always thinking of you; love your biggest fan.]

"You know you've got pics of the accident?" Caitlin asked.

Cold wiggled down Geneva's spine. *Is this another email?* She replayed Caitlin's words. "Uh, I think I shifted the camera mode by accident."

"I know I shouldn't be impressed with the clarity of your photography, but you do better than most sighted people. I have yet to find a picture of someone decapitated."

It was an email. What concerned Geneva was the line about the person being inside. Had someone been inside her house? The thought sent a chill through her.

"Geneva? Are you all right? You're really pale."

"Yes. I've been getting some weird emails lately." She printed the message before she deleted the email.

"You seem to get a surge of them after an appearance. Make sure you keep track of the emails. If they escalate, let me know so we can get the authorities involved."

Geneva nodded. "Right." Unease clung to her. "What were you asking me?"

"Oh. I was complimenting you on your photography skills. Everyone has their heads."

Geneva laughed, relieved to have something else to focus on. "All I do is listen to the prompts."

"You have a really good sense of your surroundings." Caitlin typed a few keys. "I've got the pictures uploaded in the spots you indicated. What else do you have for me?"

"Awesome. Since I have you here, how about uploading a few more? That way, I can get the rest of the month scheduled."

"Oh, sure. I'm finishing up the captions for each of the pictures in case you want to switch something out."

Geneva continued setting up her phone, logging into various apps and making sure they were synced with external storage. She was logging into her social media accounts when Caitlin gasped.

"Is something wrong?" Geneva asked.

"One of the figurines is missing."

Geneva turned in her chair in the direction of the shelving unit which hosted the little baubles. "Oh. Are you sure?"

The table creaked as the chair scraped back. Footsteps faded on the wood floor.

Caitlin responded, "Yes. There is definitely one missing."

Geneva got up to see for herself. With deliberate care, she skimmed her fingertips over the surface. A three-inch gap sat between the butterfly and the teddy bear. "Are you sure it isn't under the shelf?" Heat rose in Geneva's cheeks as she thought of the picnic and post-picnic fun she and Jethro had had.

Caitlin, who had been kneeling on the floor, stood with a grunt. "Nope."

I was inside. I was inside—the words looped through Geneva's brain.

"Hold on a moment. When was your cleaning service here?" Caitlyn asked.

Geneva thought for a moment. "They would've been here yesterday morning. We've used them for years."

"Oh no. I didn't mean to sound like I was accusing your cleaning service of anything. I was thinking they'd missed some footprints. And there are smudges of color on the windowsill."

Geneva turned abruptly and walked to her office.

"Did I say something wrong?"

With rising trepidation, Geneva walked into the office and straight to the printer. Only one sheet waited in the tray. She knew she'd printed out the first email, yet it wasn't here. *Did Jethro put it away for me?*

She went to her desk. The chair wasn't beneath the desk as she'd left it. The drawers weren't closed either.

"You're shaking!" Caitlin exclaimed in alarm. "What is it?"

"Read this?" She thrust the sheet at Caitlin. "This is the third or fourth email I've received."

Paper rattled as it exchanged hands.

What if the emails are correct? What if someone has been in my home?

"Do you have others?" Caitlin demanded.

Geneva sat in the chair, opened the bottom drawer. She thumbed through the files until she came across the one marked Looney. She handed the file to Caitlin. "I started keeping them just in case."

"They're not all from the same sender," Caitlin murmured. "I'm going to separate the ones from the same sender, then you and I are going through the house to see if anything is missing."

If she hadn't been sitting, Geneva would've fallen. "I should call Jethro. He needs to know." Her hands fluttered over the smooth surface of the desk, searching for her phone. Belatedly, she remembered it was in the dining room. "Are you sure we're not overreacting?" Geneva asked.

"Let's err on the side of caution. You were mugged. Maybe the same person who stole your phone also got into the house." Papers rustled. "I've separated the emails. Did anything strange happen at the picnic?"

"Other than a woman being hit by a car?" Geneva asked dryly.

"Right," Caitlin conceded. "Did anyone stand out to you? Seemed overly friendly or aggressive?"

Geneva shook her head, her hair whipping about her face. "No. Nothing like that. It was an idyllic afternoon."

Fingers tapped keys.

"What are you doing? Are you looking for more emails?"

"I, uh, no," Caitlin sputtered. "Still going through the pictures."

Geneva turned in Caitlin's direction. Geneva heard something odd in Caitlin's voice. "Did you find a decapitated subject or someone glaring at me?"

Caitlin's laugh seemed forced. "When I come across one, I'll let you know." There was more typing. "There we go," she announced with what sounded like forced cheer. "All fixed."

"What'd you do? Accidentally delete something?" she teased.

"Almost, but I caught it before I did."

Is that a note of relief in Caitlin's voice?

"C'mon. Let's see if there's anything else missing."

Chapter Seven

Odd, inexpensive, personal things were missing. Geneva sat on one corner of the couch, arms wrapped around her bent knees. She hadn't misplaced her body wash or nightshirt. Someone had taken them, along with a silver cuff bracelet, a pair of dangly earrings, and her favorite outfit. *Bottom line? Someone has been in my house. Someone violated my home.*

"How could someone have gotten in?" Geneva mused. "We lock our doors. There's a neighborhood patrol."

Jethro rested a hand on her knee. "It's more than that. Someone is targeting you," he said gently. "The personal items taken... that's someone fixated on you. Like a stalker."

"How could someone get into our home?" She couldn't keep the tears from sliding down her cheeks. First, someone mugged her. Now someone had broken into their home and stolen things. *My things.* "Are you sure the officer said we were safe here?"

"Yes. They're also going to have someone patrol the area every twenty minutes. I also put in a call to Dicky's A/V. They've agreed to put cameras in for us. They'll be here tomorrow afternoon."

"You know someone killed the owner?" she muttered.

"I do. The son is really good, and he has a mom who's visually impaired. So, he knows what to expect."

"I don't know. Maybe we should just move."

Jethro moved closer, pulling her reluctant body into his lap. "This is scary. Believe me, my heart is still pounding. But I'm not letting anyone run us from our home. This is our home!"

She heard the vehemence in his voice and felt it in the secure way he held her. "For the first time in my life, I'm afraid of something," she admitted. "I don't like it."

"We'll get a dog and an alarm if that's what it takes to help you feel safer. Some alarms even come with panic buttons you can keep on your person. And I can work from home for a few days."

And he would. Oddly touched, Geneva kissed Jethro's cheek. "All right. But you have to be here with me when the camera people are here installing the alarm."

"Deal."

She shifted on his lap. "I'm still uneasy. How did this person know where we live? I don't record or take pictures here at the house. And I even turn off the location tracking when I do take videos and such."

"I don't know, sweetheart. What I do know is we will make sure all doors and windows are locked before we go to bed tonight."

"All right."

A knock sounded on the door, and Geneva stiffened. Jethro gave her a quick squeeze before sliding her to the cushions.

"I'll get it," Jethro said.

A moment later, he returned with the newcomer. "I'm sorry to disturb you guys," the woman began.

"Caitlin?"

"Yes. With everything that happened, I forgot to ask if you wanted me to run you to the grocery store? Kinda like giving the middle finger to whoever this is. Showing them that they can't scare you."

Geneva chuckled. "That's really nice of you."

Shuffling feet met Geneva's ears.

Caitlin said, "Well, you're strong, and we girls got to stick together."

Geneva stood. *They are right. Caitlin and Jethro. One person wouldn't stop my world from turning.* "You're right. Both of you. I can't stop living my life." She walked to the hall table and picked up her bag. "It will be nice to squeeze my own fruit." *But I will be cautious. I will pay attention to my surroundings and the people in them.* "Do you want anything?"

Jethro leaned down and kissed her cheek. "Ice cream."

"Excellent idea. We'll have sundaes for dessert. I'll make pasta when I get back." With that, she and Caitlin left the house.

Serefina sat in her car at the end of the cul-de-sac. She kept one eye on the front door of Geneva's house while scrolling through the pictures she'd taken the other day. Every chance she got, Serefina looked at the pictures from the White Cane Event. There were a lot of Geneva and anyone who interacted with her. Serefina tried to crop those pictures, so only Geneva remained in the frame.

Pursing her lips, she swiped right and left, trying to decide which picture would make the best phone screensaver.

A flash of something caught Serefina's eye. She stopped at a photo of her and Geneva just before the accident. There was a man. She'd seen him before.

Voices drew her attention from the small screen in the house across the street.

Phone forgotten, Serefina watched the two women leave the house. She kept her gaze trained on Geneva. *Does Geneva know I was in the house? Maybe she does.* Serefina hadn't left a mess. Serefina sniffed the enduring scent of plum and honey-scented lotion on her arm. She slouched down in her seat as the two women drove past. *Where are they going?*

Serefina maneuvered her vehicle until she could follow the little VW. Just in time, too, as a police car drove by. *Did Geneva call the police?*

Serefina wiped her sweaty palm on her jeans. *No, no, no. I didn't want to frighten Geneva. I just want to be like her. Maybe I can explain.*

Chapter Eight

Mr. VIP stared through a magnifying glass at the open letter on the table. This was the final paperwork he needed regarding the dissolution of his business. He rubbed his hands together.

Years of hard work, stress, blood, and sweat would all be gone at the flick of someone's pen. *One decision. One lousy decision, and my business is gone. Not just my business, but my life, my legacy, and my daughter's inheritance.*

If I could forgive, it would change nothing! He shoved the pages away from him. Glass tinkled as it broke on the floor. A couple of flat boxes fell over.

Skirting a few boxes already packed and ready for movers, he stalked to a shelf where his wedding photo held prominence. He picked up the heavy frame and hurled it across the room. *She is the reason my business failed. I trusted her with the accounting.*

All those years he toiled to provide her with a cushy lifestyle, she was screwing another man. She took Mr. VIP's money and invested it in someone else's business venture.

Well, I made sure that man paid.

And why did she do what she did? Because of my vision. Because I am legally blind.

I could still do my damn job. I could still run my business, but she made me an outcast. Ruined my good name. The name I'd spent years building. She'd bankrupted my business and made my dreams worthless. All because I have a little visual impairment.

So, now, I have to eradicate all people like me. No one should have to suffer such setbacks. No one should have their success ripped away unless I am the one doing the ripping.

Don't my colleagues know it is simpler to be helpless and allow others to cater to us rather than have our independence snatched away with a careless scribble of ink?

He went through the room, hurling against the wall the knickknacks his wife left behind.

Just as breaking glass and bottles in Abigail's bar purged Mr. VIP's anger, so did breaking the little ceramic or crystal baubles.

Chest heaving from effort, Mr. VIP stood in the middle of the destruction. He felt calmer. When his wife, now ex, learned of Dicky's death, he could hardly contain the sense of satisfaction. Her lover's death would linger for a long time. Probably as long as the loss of his business and home. *Well, I could get another home, even another business, but she can't get another man like Dicky.*

He snorted as he crunched across glass to retrieve the broom and dustpan. He had sold the more valuable home furnishings. All that remained was his trustee barcalounger and an old sofa the real estate agent brought in for staging.

About a week after Dicky's death, Winnie came begging Mr. VIP to take her back. By then, it was too late. They were already divorced, and no amount of pleading would make him take her back, not after how she'd dismissed him.

He swept shards into the dustpan and dumped them in the trash.

She'd even asked if he had something to do with the man's death. Mr. VIP laughed in her face. Even if he'd confessed, she wouldn't have believed him. No one would believe a legally blind man could be capable of murder.

His wife hadn't thought him capable of finding out about her affairs and thievery. Now he'd begun something he didn't think he could stop. Taking the lives of successful business owners was almost an addiction. Terrorizing his colleagues was a sense of pride. *I want—*

No, I need to get rid of one of them.

I have to let blind people know that they needed to sit down somewhere and shut up. I have to let them know they don't belong in society. It doesn't matter what laws are introduced or how much technology is on their side. They all needed to be rounded up and destroyed. Why maintain independence when it could so easily be snatched away? Why work so hard to fit into a sighted world when that world clearly didn't want to be bothered?

Another pan of shards went into the trash.

Of course, I need to get rid of Geneva, and I will do that. He stopped sweeping, and a sneer curled his lips. *What better way to get rid of the blind than to start with those who would advocate for them?*

With the last bits of glass removed, Mr. VIP ran a damp mop over the area to pick up any remaining slivers.

He would take a moment and figure out how to rid the world of Murphy Giles.

Chapter Nine

Swift Time sat across from a man in a wheelchair. The man's pasty face and sandy blond hair were the only things that Time could see. "So, how have you been, Murphy?"

"I finally got the airport transportation board to understand what we need as far as assistance. There will be no more of those with service animals having to pass through security a second time. There will be a designated person to escort the handler and their guide to spot outside and then escort him back." His deep voice resonated through the open space. "At least until they can get a relief area."

"A relief area would be good. Some airports have their own doggy bathroom," Time replied.

"What can I do for you, Time?"

"I was in the neighborhood and thought I'd check in on you."

Murphy sighed. "Don't bring your woo-woo talk here."

Time laughed. "I would never bring anything like that to you. I did want to give you a warning."

Murphy sat forward. "Did you warn Abigail her place would be vandalized?" he demanded hotly. "You could've saved her thousands of dollars of damage. Did you warn Geneva she would be assaulted?"

"Murphy." Time barely kept his tone civil. "I can only share what I've been given. I warned Geneva to be careful. If I'd been given anything about Abigail, I'd have told her."

"Spare me your ramblings, old man."

Swift Time stared at him a moment. "Are you having a bad day, Murphy? Did something go wrong you want to share? You're grumpier than usual."

Murphy gaped.

"Perhaps I could get you something to drink," said Time.

Color stained Murphy's cheeks. "I suppose my words were harsh."

"Very."

Murphy heaved several breaths before he spoke again. "The State is considering not funding my position next year," he admitted dully. "If that happens, who will speak up for us?"

Time smiled. "Would you really let something like a lack of funding stop you from speaking out?" he countered. "I think if you, as well as others, spoke up loud and often enough, someone somewhere will find the money for your position or else you'll still advocate in another way."

"You're right. They can't silence me."

Time stood. "Now, be vigilant. We need more people like you who are willing to speak up and out. Give those a voice who can't speak for themselves." He stopped at the door. "Will you be at the social?"

"Of course."

"Great. See you there."

Mr. VIP waited until Time left the building. Mr. VIP checked his watch, bringing the device close to his ear to hear the time. Murphy wouldn't be much longer. Mr. VIP would catch him on a break. He thought to get rid of him at the social the next night. *But now will be better. Now would be splashier.*

He patted the pocket with the pre-filled syringe. His colleagues were so trusting and accommodating at these socials. They gave everyone free rein in their kitchens and bathrooms. *One can find so many useful things in refrigerators and medicine cabinets.*

This syringe was special. Mr. VIP been saving it for someone else but decided it would do very well for Murphy. And it would make the hospital staff think.

He walked through the steps in his head. First, he would stun Murphy. Just a quick jolt, and then he would inject the insulin under Murphy's tongue. The man would die waiting on his transportation.

The electric whine of a small motor echoed off the walls of the garage.

Another ten minutes went by. Mr. VIP leaned against a wide pillar out of sight. Mr. VIP ambushed Murphy as he passed.

A soft grunt was all he got. As soon as Murphy's head lolled to one side, Mr. VIP pulled the syringe from his pocket and thumbed off the cap. He pried open the man's mouth, lifted his tongue, and stabbed the needle home. He depressed the plunger.

Mr. VIP grimaced as Murphy's teeth snapped shut. The needle snapped, and he pulled his gloved fingers free.

Wheels crunched on cement. Mr. VIP didn't have time to retrieve the tip of the needle. Instead, he hurried away, peeled off his gloves, and wrapped them around the spent needle. He shoved the entire bundle in his pocket. He didn't want the driver to see him, so Mr. VIP ducked into the stairwell. He went up a level, found an exit, and walked away.

I did it. I got rid of Murphy Giles. Now, to get rid of the next.

Geneva sat at her desk, exploring the options on a pen-sized device. The device used special stickers on which recipes, instructions, or short notes could be stored and played back.

She didn't see how this differed from other items already on the market, but she'd give it a shot.

The rich scent of chili, onion, and tomatoes filled the air. Geneva would give this article another ten minutes, and then she needed to make cornbread for dinner.

A door slammed, and hurried footsteps dragged her attention from her computer.

"Geneva."

She turned in her chair, annoyed at being interrupted. "What? I'm almost done."

"Honey, Murphy Giles is dead."

She shook her head. She saw him the other day at the White Cane Event and again at the wrestling match. "What? Are you sure?"

He grasped her hands. "Yes. He was found unresponsive by the paratransit driver, and he died on the way to the hospital."

"But how?"

"They think it was a heart attack."

Even though she found Giles boisterous and tedious, the man had helped her when she struggled with transportation through the paratransit program.

"This has been a very sucky week," said Geneva.

Jethro leaned his forehead against hers. "Tell me about it."

"If I were paranoid, I'd say someone has it out for small business owners and those of us in the blind community."

"Why would you say that?"

She shook her head and sighed. "Did you know three small business owners have died since the beginning of the year?"

"A lot of people have died since the beginning of the year," Jethro pointed out.

"Well, two deaths, a mugging, and Abigail's business all happened this week. Do you think those are coincidences?"

"I think you may be a little sensitive to what's going on because of what happened at the event and your own assault," he said carefully.

"What if I tell you Penelope and Amelia were attacked in some way?"

"Someone was after Amelia's money, and someone wanted to force Penelope into selling her family bakery." Jethro cupped her face. "That doesn't mean someone is out to get the blind community."

She shook off his hands and stood. "It makes sense the more I think about it."

"So why would someone want to hurt us?"

"I don't know. We're productive citizens of society. Small businesses provide many jobs in the area. Why do people normally hurt one another?" Since she was up, she went to make the cornbread.

"Jealousy, envy, greed," Jethro offered.

"Who would be jealous of us?" Geneva went straight for the oven and turned it to 400 degrees. Next, she grabbed a mixing bowl and the ingredients for cornbread. "We work twice as hard as everybody else just to appear normal."

"Other blind people could be jealous."

Egg in hand, she gaped. "Seriously?"

"Why not. The person sees we're thriving, adapting, and overcoming a challenge, and well, maybe they can't or are unwilling to put in the same amount of work."

"Huh," she pondered as she cracked the egg into the bowl and followed it with milk and oil.

"Something to think about, right?" Jethro crossed to the stove, lifted the lid on the simmering pot, and stirred.

"It is." Geneva mixed the ingredients until the mixture was thick and a little lumpy. She poured the batter into a waiting pan. She hip bumped Jethro away from the stove. "Leave the chili until the bread is done," she admonished.

"But it smells so good." He waited until she'd slid the pan in the oven and closed the door before he wrapped his arms around her waist. He pulled her close. "How did you and Caitlin get along today?"

"She labeled all the pics I took over the last few days and uploaded the ones I wanted to the website."

He rubbed his chin on the top of her head. "And what did you think of that nifty little device? That pen scanner thing."

"There are better ones on the market, but I haven't gotten to play with all the features yet."

A xylophone-like chime filled the air. "Hold that thought, love," Jethro said. "My phone is ringing."

Geneva listened as his footsteps faded. She went around the kitchen, readying the table with placemats, bowls, and silverware. She had time to think about Murphy Giles.

The man will be deeply missed. His opinions and loud voice could be obnoxious, but his advocacy for the blind and disabled came from the heart. Our meetings and gatherings will be a lot quieter without him.

She was just placing the finished cornbread on a plate when Jethro returned to the kitchen.

"They're still going ahead with the social gathering tomorrow. They're gonna use it as a wake of sorts."

"I don't know." She still had some reservations about leaving the house. Even her small foray to the grocery store left her a little anxious. As if sensing her thoughts, Jethro covered her hand.

"I'll be with you, Geneva."

She blinked back hot tears. "Is it that obvious?"

"Anyone would be a little nervous after being mugged." He ladled chili into waiting bowls. "It's a very human reaction."

She leaned over and kissed him. "Thank you."

Chapter Ten

Rodney shuffled through the drawer of the side table he kept in his front foyer. The thing had to be here. He shoved mittens, old mail, and scarves aside in his search. With a huff, he shoved the drawer shut. He opened the one below it and repeated the same process.

Stepping back, he ran his fingers through his hair. *Where did I put my cane?* He moved to the hall closet. Maybe it was in one of his pockets. *Of course, I have more than one cane, but that is my favorite.*

Bing, bong, ding, dong chimed through the house. Mr. VIP stepped from the closet and closed the door. *Who in the world is visiting me?* He didn't think he had any other packages scheduled for delivery, and he wasn't expecting company. With a deep breath, he walked toward the front door.

"Who is it?" he called, standing to one side of the wood. He didn't bother with the peephole. The lens distorted the faces too much for him to recognize.

"Geneva. Geneva Martin," came the reply.

Oh, this is way too easy. Geneva paying me a house call? He looked over his shoulder at the array of boxes and packing materials. All that remained was to clean out the front closet and little side table. How was he going to explain the mess? He remembered Geneva wouldn't be able to see anything in his home. Mr. VIP scratched his head. *What does she want?* There was only one way to find out. He opened the door. He plastered what he hoped was a genial smile on his face.

At first glance, he thought it was Geneva. He recognized the pale green blouse and patterned skirt. The scent of plums and honey tickled his nostrils, but he noticed she'd done something different to her hair. It wasn't curly or straight. The woman looked him in the eye. It was not Geneva.

"Who the hell are you?" he demanded.

She smiled. "I told you. I'm Geneva."

Mr. VIP moved to close the door. She shoved him back, knocking him off balance.

He grabbed the wall and managed to remain upright. "Geneva" slipped in and locked the door.

"You are not Geneva," he snapped, just a little unnerved at this woman's boldness.

She frowned. "But of course I am. I look just like her."

Mr. VIP folded his arms across his chest. "You have eyes."

"It's a shame, really. Geneva has such an amazing world. Did you know you can smell and taste colors?" She ran an index finger along the patterned wall.

Mr. VIP watched as "Geneva" traced the stenciled swirls and whirls. He'd seen her before. He squinted. *Ah! That was it. The coffee shop.*

"Are you following me?" he demanded.

She smiled, but somehow it looked wrong to Mr. VIP. The lips curved, but not the eyes. "I saw you," she said.

He scoffed. "Apparently, you need help. I suggest you get some."

"I saw you push down a blind woman and steal her bag."

Heart pounding a little faster, he gave the woman his full attention. "You are mistaken."

She smiled again. There was no humor or warmth behind the smile. She began, "I saw you. You went into a coffeeshop."

Apprehension gnawed at his insides. *How should I play this? Should I go on the defensive or wait until she says something more?* He decided to play clueless. "Maybe I missed something. I frequent a few of the coffee shops in the area. To which are you referring? If you can provide me with a name, I can tell you whether or not I was there." *That should take care of her.*

She laughed, a light, hearty sound that reminded him of youth, vitality, and invincibility.

"Oh no. Nothing like that." She fumbled in a pocket and removed a phone. "What's that saying? A picture's worth a thousand words."

Mr. VIP stiffened as she held out the device. He feigned nonchalance as he accepted the device. His hands were steady, but his pulse raced, and his heart pounded. He was surprised she couldn't see or hear his heart's frantic gallop.

He didn't have to raise the phone to see the back of his body, foot raised, and something glinting on the pavement. She had a picture of him. And anyone with a brain would be able to see this was him.

"I deduced." She smiled again. "Isn't that a great word? I deduced there was something on Geneva's phone, and you couldn't find it."

He shrugged. "So what?"

She retraced the paint patterns. "That got me thinking. Geneva would never know who hurt her. You see, I love Geneva. She's my absolute idol, and I'd do anything for her."

VIP kept one eye on the phone and the other on the girl. "So, you have a photo of me stomping a phone. Big deal." He held out the phone.

"Oh. I've got more than that." She pulled another phone from her pocket. This one was an older iPhone.

VIP eyed it warily.

"Why would a man, especially one I saw Geneva talking to, want to hurt her? It's not like she can actually see all the photos she's taken." She wiggled the phone. "Go ahead. Look. I know you want to."

VIP snatched the phone away. He didn't have far to look. There it was. Nothing. He allowed his shoulder to sag. He'd planned to kill Geneva, and now he didn't have to.

Tears burned his eyes. Geneva had seen him at his lowest point. *How could I ever have thought about killing her? And now, this Geneva wannabe is standing in my foyer staring at me with open speculation.* He tossed the iPhone at her.

She caught it deftly in one hand and smiled.

"I was there that day." She tucked the phone back in her pocket. "I will never forget the White Cane Event. It was the day I met Geneva." She cast a dreamy, faraway look. "Did you know she hugged me? She even put me on her website."

He moved toward the door. "All right. It's time you left. You've worn out your welcome."

"Geneva takes a lot of pictures," she continued conversationally. "It was careless of you to throw away the phone like that. Had you been thinking, you could've done the same thing I did."

His gaze dropped to the phone she held in her hand. Realization dawned. *Stupid. I've been stupid.* She'd retrieved the SIM card and somehow managed to gain access to Geneva's entire phone. *And yes, had I been thinking instead of reacting, I'd have been able to do the same thing. After all, that was part of my business.*

He felt rather than saw her shift. "You changed her password."

Now, the smile lit her eyes. "Absolutely." Now her tone turned sly. "There was an accident at the White Cane event."

"Of course. I was there. A woman died."

"Did you have something to do with her death?" Fake Geneva challenged.

Sweat rolled down his back and pooled at his waistband. "I don't think I like your tone," he said defensively. Geneva had captured his misdeeds on her camera, and this woman had seen it. *But if Geneva doesn't know what she has, is it possible for me to grab her other devices? Maybe it would be more prudent to upload a worm to her network. Had I thought about that, instead of destroying her phone, this smug young woman wouldn't be hassling me.* "What a positively despicable thing to say." He turned to the door. "I'd like you to leave now."

"Aren't you even curious as to what I have?" She leaned forward. "I couldn't have you hurting Geneva. She's simply the absolute, magarrific best. So, all the pictures that showed you doing some truly naughty things, I erased from all her devices and the cloud."

"Young lady, I've had enough of you!"

Fake "Geneva" shoved the phone in VIP's face. He grabbed her wrist, snatched the device, and studied the photo. It was blurred, but enough of his arm showed that he was aiming something into Sherry's face. *Will this be enough to incriminate me?* He stared at the screen long after the light dimmed. If this "Geneva" wannabe made him out, so would someone else.

He locked the door and pocketed the phone.

"Hey! Give that back."

Mr. VIP pushed his glasses farther up his nose. "No. I'm afraid I can't do that." He moved forward as she stumbled back.

Her eyes went from triumph to terror. "Stay away from me." She darted around a stack of boxes.

Mr. VIP moved with her.

She shoved a stack at him. He barely missed being hit. The contents in the cardboard box fell to the floor.

Mr. VIP kicked the bubble-wrapped dishes aside. Fake "Geneva" darted into the tiny living room and put a chair between them. "Stay away."

Does she really think a crappy piece of furniture will stop me? He shoved the chair, trapping her against the wall. He picked up a nearby pillow.

"I'm sorry about this. Really, I am." He held the pillow over her face.

Serefina had been so confident she could get what she wanted. Finding Mr. VIP hadn't been hard, not when Geneva kept meticulous contact records. All Serefina had to do was scroll through the address book and find Mr. VIP, whose contact pic was a photo of his face. Geneva knew VIP and loved going to his shop. He probably didn't even remember her. When she was in high school, she interned at his shop. Ten years later, his shop was no more, and she had pictures proving he was a murderer.

Now, Serefina was trying to stay alive. She ran farther into the apartment, hoping for another exit—a balcony, patio, anything to get away from this man. Colors flashed as she searched for a hiding spot. She ran behind an armchair. If she could make it to the couch, she could circle back and go out the front door. She stumbled.

Mr. VIP rammed the chair into her. Serefina gasped. She couldn't move. He had pinned one of her arms against the wall, and she couldn't get enough leverage to push the chair away.

She stared into Mr. VIP's eyes. She saw them sparkle with anticipation, and if she wasn't mistaken, excitement. In that instant, she knew she was going to die. There would be no hysterics. She would not beg. She closed her eyes.

The scent of plums, lavender, and honey engulfed her. Ozone and pine tried to drown out the plums. A simultaneously rough and soft fabric pressed against her face. If this were her final act of love for Geneva, she would meet death with her head held high.

She had to draw breath, but no air entered her lungs. Blackness closed around her, and she dug her fingers in the wall at her back. The plaster was cool. The same swirls and whirls greeted her fingers. The heavy press of the soft chair held her upright.

I am Geneva. No one can take that from me again.

Chapter Eleven

Going back out into the world wasn't as bad as Geneva thought it would be. The first venture had been to the grocery store with Caitlin. Thankfully, no one in the grocery store approached them. Or if they had, Caitlin kept them at bay. On the second outing, Caitlin, Geneva, and Jethro walked to Abigail's place.

On any other night, the music would have been loud and fast. Voices, TV, and the occasional grind of blenders would all be vying for attention. There was none of that. The bar was so quiet that laughter, steam, and sizzling sounds spilled from the kitchen.

"Where is everyone?" she whispered, unwilling to breach the silence.

Jethro chuckled. "We're not in a library. You don't have to whisper."

"Oh." Heat filled her cheeks as she realized what she'd done.

"It looks like she's closed to the public." He clicked his tongue, then shifted their movements more to the right.

Their footsteps echoed back, and Geneva realized they were in the corridor moving toward kitchen noises and the banquet rooms.

"I'm glad you forced me to come out," she told Jethro as she clutched his biceps.

He patted her hand. "It will get better. We will both rest easier when the intruder is caught." He clicked his mouth again. They stopped, and Jethro pushed open a door. Muted conversation spilled out. "After you."

Geneva maneuvered inside, her cane sweeping back and forth. "Hi everyone. It's Geneva and Jethro," said Geneva.

Chairs scraped, and shoes scuffed on the floor. "It's me, Penelope." She hugged Geneva. "How are you?" asked Penelope

"I'm okay."

"If you ever need to talk, let me know," said Penelope.

Geneva squeezed her hand. "I will. Was Avery able to make it tonight?"

Penelope laughed. "You know he doesn't like to let me out of his sight. He says I get into trouble."

"I heard that," came Avery's dulcet tones. "And you do." He patted Geneva on the shoulder. "Loved the shots and videos you uploaded to your website. Thanks for the nod to the bakery."

Geneva grinned. "You guys have the best pastries in the city."

"Aw, thanks." Penelope squeezed her hand. "We'll talk later." Penelope and Avery's footsteps receded.

"Who else is here?" Geneva asked as she leaned into Jethro.

"I'm not sure."

She stiffened against him.

He trailed gentle fingers down the curve of her cheek. "We're among friends. There's no one here out to hurt you."

"I know. It's a mental thing."

He kissed her forehead. "All right, sweetheart. I'll sit you near Avery and Penelope. Oh, I see Joshua and Amelia. You'll be safe near them."

"Oh, good. I wanted to talk with Joshua and Amelia. I think one way to combat my fear is to learn self-defense."

Jethro hugged her tightly. "I think that's a great idea! I would be interested in learning some moves myself."

Hinges creaked behind them. "Rodney just walked in," said Jethro.

"I want to talk to him too. You know just to make sure he's okay. He's lost a lot these past several months."

Jethro was so close now his lips brushed her ear. His warm breath tickled and teased. "His wife did him a real disservice. If we ever fall out of love and you no longer want me, I hope you tell me."

She reached up to keep him near and kissed him. "I promise I will, but I don't see me falling out of love with you until we're both too old to have picnics on the living room floor."

Jethro kissed her again. Catcalls and whistles made Geneva's cheeks blush. "I forgot we weren't alone," she murmured.

"I did too," he said sheepishly.

"It's great to see love in action," Avery commented. "Murphy would've approved."

"Here. Here!" the group chorused.

As if a dam burst, music floated in from hidden speakers. A mellow tune by Michael McDonald, one of Murphy's favorite artists, filled the air.

Jethro guided Geneva to a chair against the wall between Joshua and Avery. "Keep an eye on my best girl until I get back," Jethro said to the two men. He turned, and his clicking tongue faded into the music.

Clothing rustled on her left as a chair scraped. "Did I overhear you say you're interested in taking self-defense?" Joshua Hasting's southern drawl reminded Geneva of humid lazy nights.

"You did. Could you?"

"Absolutely!" he leaned closer. "And I can show you a few things you can do with your cane."

"Really?"

"It's empowering!" Amelia chimed in. "Just think what it will look like on your website."

Footsteps shuffled, and dog-tags jangled. "I suppose this is where all the cool kids are?" Abigail teased.

"Oh, sure. Come join us," Geneva invited.

The table wobbled when Abigail sat. "I can't stay too long. Gotta check on the food. They'll be bringing it out in a bit."

Geneva heard clicking and ice cubes softly tinkling against glasses. "You made it." She couldn't keep the breathless relief from her voice.

"I think you missed me." Jethro placed the glasses on the table, then sat in the vacant chair next to Geneva.

Under the table, she twined her fingers with his. His palm was cold and a little damp against her warmer hand. He squeezed back, and she relished how just holding his hand could bring her such comfort.

"Hello, Abigail," Jethro said. He turned to Geneva and said, "Your glass is near your right hand."

"Thanks," she murmured.

Abigail turned her unseeing gaze on him. "Jethro. One of my employees said Geneva was attacked. You should've come by and told me."

"I didn't even think about it."

"It happened the same day as someone busted up the bar." Abigail sighed. "I don't know what's going on right now. First, it was the woman at the event, then my bar, then Geneva, and now Murphy." She sniffled. "I can't believe he's gone."

"I think everyone here has a Murphy story," Jethro said.

"That's why I wanted it to be just us. Murphy's family is planning the wake and funeral, but he'd have liked for us to celebrate his life. With food, music, and plenty of alcohol."

The squeak of sneakers grew loud. "Abigail. You're needed," a feminine voice said.

Abigail stood. "Duty calls."

As she left, Geneva leaned toward Jethro. "Where's Rodney?"

"Not sure." Jethro shifted in his chair, his knee brushing hers.

"He's in the far corner," Avery said helpfully. "I think he's speaking to one of Murphy's children."

Geneva pushed her chair back and stood. She was familiar enough with the room to make her way to the far table.

A hint of gasoline and the faintest whiff of burnt wood greeted her. "Rodney?"

A chair scraped, and a soft hand touched her arm. "And what did I do to deserve your company?" Rodney greeted.

Despite the smile in his voice, Geneva heard an undercurrent of sadness. "I just wanted to check on you."

"Of course. Oh, and I also wanted to show you the pictures. See if there are any from the event you'd like me to send you."

Silence met her statement. He was quiet for so long. She thought he might have walked away.

"Rodney?"

Fabric brushed her arm, and the scent of gas intensified before dispelling. She wrinkled her nose and shifted. "I've got my phone if you're interested."

A chuckle reached her ears. "Of course. I've time to look. Maybe you have some of me and Murphy?" Rodney responded.

Geneva nodded. "I'm sure I do. Caitlin labeled all of them for me, so I would know who's in them and vaguely know what's going on."

The phone squished and talked as Geneva swiped. She then turned her attention to the waitstaff.

"If I could have your attention for a moment," Abigail called over the din. "Kyle here will go through the goodies we have."

Rodney nudged Geneva. "There are two of me with Murphy. Both are under the banner. I'd like those."

Geneva focused on Rodney and made a voice note. "You got it."

"You really are a wonderful person."

Surprised by the depth of emotion, Geneva gave him a quick hug. He winced as she released him. "Did I hurt you?"

"Not at all. I slipped in the shower and am still a little sore."

"I'm sorry. And I'm squeezing you like a lemon."

"Here, let me walk you back to your table. They're serving food."

Before they could cross the room, clicking reached her ears. Geneva smiled. "No worries. Here's Jethro."

"Hey, Rodney!" Jethro stated. "You are looking well."

"Kind of you to say so." Rodney's soft voice was his most distinctive characteristic. Geneva didn't think she'd ever heard him raise his voice.

"You are a truly a lucky man. I hope my daughter can be like Geneva," said Rodney.

"Thanks, man," replied Jethro.

"Well, I'll leave you two to it. I'm gonna grab a plate before it's all gone."

Geneva tried listening for his footsteps, but the raised voices, and a burst of laughter drowned them out.

Geneva and Jethro were nearly back to their table when a thunderclap shook the building. A few people screamed, and the room fell into an uneasy silence.

"What was that?" someone asked.

"Holy moly," someone else muttered.

A smaller explosion rolled through the building. "Cripes."

Geneva clung to Jethro.

"Is someone shooting off firecrackers?" Penelope asked.

"Those weren't firecrackers," came Joshua's slow drawl. "I'll see what's going on."

Before he could move, the door smacked the wall.

"Oh, good. Everyone is safe!"

"Brian?" Abigail raised her voice.. "What's happening?"

"Car crash. It exploded and set two more vehicles on fire. They're asking everyone to stay inside and off the street."

Mr. VIP nibbled a carrot as he watched the flicker of orange and yellow. He sat at the farthest table at the back of Abigail's place. His choice of seating allowed him an unobstructed yet blurry view of the street. *I almost made a mistake. I almost killed Geneva.*

The world is brighter with her in it. Mr. VIP shifted his gaze to observe Geneva smiling up at her husband. They really did make a cute couple. A twinge of guilt of what he'd nearly done stabbed at him. Jethro was good. He didn't deserve for VIP to rip his world apart. Jethro was visually disabled too.

He picked up a wing and bit off a chunk. The spicy buffalo burned his nose and tongue. He wouldn't hurt anyone if they were in a same relationship—two visually impaired people. But if it was a mixed relationship—a sighted person with a visually disabled one, the bets were off. He eyed Amelia and Penelope for a long moment. He'd have to come back to them. Although, he didn't think he'd get another chance with them. Not when their men were so wary.

Mr. VIP returned his attention to the window. The fire still raged, casting twisted shadows and black smoke everywhere.

Fire is a rather ingenious, if slightly inconvenient, way of getting rid of lingering DNA. Since the fake "Geneva" had a car with a lithium battery, the fire would burn hot and stay hot for a long time. If it burned hot enough, the only thing left would be ashes and bone. No one would ever know she'd been in his home, especially now that he had sold his house.

Since he helped set up the surveillance in his building, he removed the sections showing her driving into the complex and walking to his apartment and the section with him leaving with her dead body and car. *And I did all that from the comfort of my easy chair.*

Thunk! Scrape.

Mr. VIP looked up to find an older black man with a shock of white hair and facial hair. Mr. VIP met and held the man's gaze. Mr. VIP saw knowledge in those deep, blue-rimmed brown irises, and it gave him an uneasy thrum in the pit of his stomach.

"Hey, Swift. How are you? I caught your match the other day," Mr. VIP began.

"Did you now?"

"You won, if I recall." Mr. VIP did not look away. He wanted to, but he couldn't. *No, I won't look away from the challenge in those too knowing eyes.*

"Do you really think you're going to get away with this?" Swift Time's voice was so low only VIP could hear.

Haven't I been through this routine already? "Get away with what?"

Swift searched his face. VIP kept his features as neutral as possible. He would not let this old man knock him off his square. Pandemonium was occurring just outside. People were celebrating the life of a man VIP had killed, and Swift Time was eyeing VIP as if he'd stepped in dog shit. A scratching noise shifted Swift's gaze down.

With two ashy fingers, Swift pushed a card no bigger than a credit card across the wooden surface. When VIP tried to take it, Swift held on.

Mr. VIP leaned forward, then jerked back. "How did…" He stopped speaking. He'd been very careful. He'd retraced his steps several times to make sure he hadn't dropped anything.

Time drew his hand back. Mr. VIP slapped his palm over Time's, preventing the man from moving.

"What do you want?" Mr. VIP demanded. His voice held a lethal edge. "If it's money you want, I ain't got it. My ex took care of that."

"Turn yourself in."

"Nobody can prove a thing." Mr. VIP leaned forward with a sly smile on his face. "You're on my list, old man. You step away, and maybe I'll let you live."

They locked gazes. Time's face lit with amusement, and Mr. VIP caught a whiff of self-doubt. Mr. VIP had taken down three so far and missed out on two. But there were still others he could get to.

"I know what you did." Time's eyes never left Mr. VIP's face. "This," Time tapped the card on the table, "will go a long way to identifying the poor woman you'd kill."

Mr. VIP released him and sat back. *How in the world am I going to get Serefina's I.D. away from Time? Actually, how am I going to eliminate Time? This old man cannot live after tonight.*

"You couldn't do it, could you?" asked Time

"Do what?"

Time tilted his head toward Geneva. "I know you mugged her."

"She's too much like my daughter," he admitted.

"Thought as much." The ID disappeared into Time's pocket. "I can't prove it now, but I will. When I do, I'm taking you down hard."

Mr. VIP snorted. "This ain't the ring, old man. Ain't nobody around here gonna chant your name to give you strength. So, old man," he leaned on the words, "go back to your rocking chair and reruns of M*A*S*H."

Time stood. With a smirk, he replied, "I'm giving you 48 hours to get your affairs in order. After that, this old man is gonna spank you like the child you are."

Mr. VIP glared after Time until he could see him no more. *How dare that man come over here and ruin my perfectly good celebration?* He drummed his fingers on the table. *How did Time get Serefina's driver's license?*

Without a word to anyone, Mr. VIP slipped from the room. He didn't think they would miss him. He would take the next 48 hours to plan, but it wasn't for flight. He was going to take down Mr. Tick Tock. That old man would regret threatening him.

Epilogue

"You mean she was the one who broke into our house?" Geneva exclaimed. "She was one of the first people to find me at the park."

Sgt. Falls shifted, his shoes creaking as if they were new. "Her husband filed a missing person's report. Coupled with what we were able to find from the wreckage." Sgt. Falls cleared his throat. "We found several of the items you listed as being missing. She had an entire room filled with pictures of you, Mrs. Martin."

Geneva sat heavily on the couch behind her. She couldn't believe the same young woman she'd met at the White Cane Awareness picnic a few short weeks ago was the same woman who broke into her home.

"What about the accident?" asked Jethro. He twined his fingers with Geneva's.

"We can't tell you much more than it's an ongoing investigation."

Geneva looked up. "Are you saying there was foul play? Serefina didn't own a small business."

Sgt. Falls cleared his throat again. "From the pictures we have of Mrs. Gellar, she resembled you quite a bit. Perhaps someone mistook her for you?"

Geneva ran through the possibilities. *Yes, more than one person sent me odd emails, but they've been checked out and dismissed as harmless.* Sgt. Falls shifted again. This time, she caught a whiff of charred wood.

"Oh no," she breathed as memories of Murphy Giles' celebration flooded her mind. "It couldn't be. But he couldn't, could he?"

"Mrs. Martin? Are you okay? Would you like my partner to get you a glass of water?"

She shook her head. "No. No, thank you. I'm fine." She snuggled closer to Jethro, who placed his arm around her shoulders and drew her even closer.

"I'm sorry we couldn't bring you better news," Sgt. Falls said. "We'll still keep the patrols going in the area. In the meantime, use your alarm system and the cameras. Talk to your neighbors. Your block seems friendly enough. Make sure you look out for one another."

"I'll see them out." Jethro patted her hand and stood.

When Jethro returned, Geneva stood in front of the stove. He came and slipped his arms around her waist. "You're still a little pale."

"I think it's Rodney."

"Think what is Rodney?" He rubbed his chin along the top of her head. A few of her hairs tangled in his beard.

She turned in his arm. "At the last social event, I smelled gas and wood smoke on Rodney."

He started to laugh and stopped. "But he was there the entire time."

She shook her head. "I know. It's silly." She wrapped her arms around his neck and allowed him to lift her off her feet. "Why don't we order in? At least we now know who was my biggest fan."

Jethro kissed her soundly before setting her back on her feet. "Yes. She was very sweet and excited to meet you. It is a real tragedy she died the way she did."

Even as they mulled over what to have for dinner, Geneva prayed she was wrong. She couldn't fathom Rodney killing her biggest fan. But there were other things to worry about.

"Hey, Jethro?"

"Yes?"

She grinned. "Do you think we should paint the nursery blue or pink?"

Author's Note

Hello, Fans and Readers.

I just wanted to pop in and give you a quick clarification about the guide dog in this book. Kiska is a fictional creation. Any trainer of guide, seeing eye, or leader dogs will tell you the animal is trained to help the blind or visually impaired navigate a sighted world. They are trained to cross streets, move us out of the path of vehicles (yes, even the electric ones), to guide us around obstacles, and keep us from falling downstairs or off curbs. This is only a fraction of what they are trained to do. Sadly, depending on your point of view, they are not trained to protect. This has been reiterated to me on numerous occasions with these wonderful trainers at Southeastern Guide Dogs, where I received my guide over two years ago.

A caveat to that is a dog is a dog. They have a fierce love and loyalty to his or her handler. While the guide may not be trained to protect, a dog's natural instinct is to protect their pack. I've witnessed this when my guide has placed himself between me and other dogs or people. Fortunately, most people I encounter are more afraid of my fur ball than he is of them. The mere sight of him is enough to scare people away.

I had fun giving Kiska a super protective and vocal personality. Hopefully, you'll love her as much as I do.

4 Horsemen Publications

Romance

Ann Shepphird
The War Council

Emily Bunney
All or Nothing
All the Way
All Night Long
All She Needs
Having it All
All at Once
All Together
All for Her

Lynn Chantale
The Baker's Touch
Blind Secrets

Mimi Francis
Private Lives
Second Chances
Run Away Home
The Professor

4HorsemenPublications.com